IGNITION
AGENTS OF ENSENADA PREQUEL

Tess Summers

Seasons Press LLC

COPYRIGHT 2020 TESS SUMMERS

Published: 2020

ISBN: 9798594753587

Published by Seasons Press LLC.

Copyright © 2020, Tess Summers.

Edited by Simone Elise

Cover by OliviaProDesign.

All rights reserved. No part of this publication may be reproduced, stored in a retrieval system, or transmitted in any form or by any means, electronic, mechanical, recording, or otherwise, without the prior written permission of the author, except in the case of brief quotations within critical reviews and otherwise as permitted by copyright law.

This is a work of fiction. The characters, incidents and dialogues in this book are of the author's imagination and are not to be construed as real. Any resemblance to actual events or persons, living or dead, is completely coincidental.

This book is for mature readers. It contains sexually explicit scenes and graphic language that may be considered offensive by some.

All sexually active characters in this work are eighteen years of age or older.

Ignition
Agents of Ensenada, Prequel

Betrayal had always been part of the plan; falling in love complicated everything.

Dante Guzman

He knew within hours that Ruby Rhodes, the sexy little auburn-haired beauty, who just happened to sit next to him at his favorite bar and flirt with him all night long, was not who she appeared to be. Redheads were his kryptonite—everyone knew it, including his enemies who wanted to see the Guzman cartel destroyed. Just exactly who sent her and why was something he was going to have to figure out. At least playing along with her was enjoyable since part of her ruse seemed to entail sleeping with him and indulging his... let's say, *darker* desires.

Or maybe that wasn't supposed to be part of the plan, and she broke the rules.

Falling in love with Ruby was definitely not part of his plan, and Dante was going to have to punish her for making him do just that. Especially after he learns who she really is and why she was sent to seduce him.

Join My Newsletter for a FREE Book

BookHip.com/SNGBXD Sign up here to receive my newsletter, and get SWAT Captain, Craig Baxter and SWAT rookie, Maddie Monroe's love story, exclusively for newsletter subscribers. You'll receive free bonus content, regular updates (but I won't bombard you with emails, I promise), and be the first to know about my works-in-progress.

Table of Contents

*I*GNITION
Tess Summers

Chapter One

Dante

It'd been a good day. He'd signed the papers on the winery—another legitimate business added to the Guzman cartel, a huge illegal shipment had made it through US customs undetected, and he'd had time to stop off for a drink at his favorite bar in downtown Ensenada before meeting Carmen for dinner. His sporadic dinners with Carmen always meant his dick was getting wet with no strings or expectations attached—and, bonus, she was usually gone from the hotel room before he even fell asleep.

Like he said, a good day.

The heavy, wooden bar door opened, allowing a summer breeze in, and he had to do a double take when the most beautiful, petite redhead he'd ever seen stepped inside wearing a simple white, sleeveless dress that highlighted her tiny waist and ample tits and hips—exactly his type. Her pale skin had just a touch of pink, like she'd gotten a little too much sun earlier, and her green eyes surveyed the bar like she owned it. The numerous shopping bags in her hands from all the local souvenir shops seemed to indicate she was a tourist—which made sense because had she been a local, he'd have known who the hell she was and would have probably tried to fuck her by now. Redheads were his kryptonite.

She made her way to the bar—the only available seats were the ones on either side of him. Most people from the community knew better than to sit next to a member of the Guzman family when they were out having a drink. The Guzmans didn't like being disturbed. But the redhead plunked her bags on the empty chair to his left and turned to him with a pleasant smile.

"Hi. Do you speak English?"

For a second, Dante considered playing dumb but found himself wanting to engage her in a conversation, so he nodded his head yes.

"Oh, good. Would you, um, mind moving one seat over, so I can sit there?" she pointed to his chair.

This was new. Nobody would ever dare ask him to move. Especially not in this town. People moved to accommodate him, not the other way around. But it wasn't like he could ask the American, "Do you know who I am?"

He watched her with a mixture of amusement at her brazenness and fascination with her beauty as she put her hands at the small of her back and pressed her chest forward, like she was stretching. The black lacy bra peeking through the opening of her blouse as the buttons stretched and the way her lips parted when she let out a small groan of relief with her eyes closed had him unable to look away. Visions of what she'd look like orgasming under him popped in his head, and his dick stirred in his pants.

"I'll buy you a drink for your trouble."

He blinked at her. Did she just suggest buying him a drink? Then he realized he hadn't moved his seat yet, and she was sweetening the deal.

"You don't have to buy me a drink," he murmured as he slid off the stool. "Are you expecting someone?"

Her smile was genuine when she hopped onto the seat he'd just occupied and turned to face him. "I insist." She was fucking adorable when she twisted back and forth on the spinning stool like a little kid. "And no, no one is joining me. I just have an aversion to leaving my bags on the floor."

Antonio, Dante's favorite bartender appeared, and she also asked him with a sweet smile, "Do you speak English?" Dante was betting that smile had bought her a lot of leniency over the years.

The man on the other side of the bar returned her smile and opened his mouth to answer in the affirmative, but Dante subtly shook his head *no* at the man. It was a goddamn tourist town—most people in the hospitality industry spoke at least a little English, enough to get by with vacationers, but for some reason, Dante wanted her to rely on him to translate.

"*Lo siento, señorita.*" Antonio replied with an apologetic smile.

"Oh, um," she bit her bottom lip nervously. "*Tee-en-ace* Macallan whiskey?" She gestured like she was doing a shot and repeated slowly, "Whiskey. Macallan."

Antonio glanced at Dante for guidance. Dante winked at him before starting his role of her translating knight in shining armor and asked the bartender her question—the one he already understood but in Spanish. The man replied—even though he knew Dante already knew the answer, and Dante looked down at her. "He says yes, but they only have Macallan Cask. It's seventy-five American dollars a shot. But they have lots of other whiskey choices, just not top shelf."

Macallan Cask was so expensive because that's what Dante drank, and the bar wanted to make sure it wasn't sold out when he came in. Plus, it was just expensive to begin with.

"Oh, wow. Is that all? I usually have to pay two hundred a shot for Macallan Cask in Houston. Can you ask him to make it a double and put it on ice?" She turned and started fishing through her purse but nodded over her shoulder toward his glass on the bar. "And put whatever you're drinking on my tab, too."

"I'm having the same thing you are."

She twisted around and looked up at him in disbelief with those emerald eyes of hers. "What? No you're not," then grabbed his drink and took a sip, her eyes widening as the liquid hit her taste buds. "You are!"

He couldn't help but grin at her. Her gumption was goddamn endearing.

"I am. And you're not buying it for me, sweetheart, but I will be paying for yours."

"Well, *sugar pie*," she mocked—he assumed at his use of the term *sweetheart*—"that's very gallant of you. Thank you."

Two doubles later, she was chattering up a storm about everything under the sun—from plastic straws to Major League Baseball to sea lions caught in fishing line discarded by fishermen. Dante just sat back, watching with amusement at how animated she got when she felt passionately about something. He could listen to her all night.

In the middle of one of her stories, she flung her hand for emphasis, sending Dante's drink into his lap.

Springing up from her seat with a horrified look on her face, she began dabbing at his lap with a napkin. "Oh, I'm so sorry." When that didn't seem to help, she rubbed his crotch frantically, muttering, "So, so sorry," as she did. His cock flexed at the motion, and he put his hand on her wrist to still her. Ruby glanced up at him with a confused look. Dante smirked and glanced down at his dick where her hand still was. Her eyes grew to the size of saucers when she realized what she'd been doing.

"Oh my god. I'm—" Her hand moved from his crotch to his forearm. "I wasn't thinking. I didn't mean to touch..." She stopped short and closed her eyes for a long minute before opening them again with a contrite smile. "I'm only making it worse, aren't I?"

Dante replied with a smirk, "Oh, I don't know. An argument could be made that you were making it *much* better before I stopped you."

His words had the intended effect because the blush started at her chest and crept up her neck all the way to her cheeks. Still, she sassily replied, "My technique is much better when there are no pants involved at all," then hopped back on her chair.

This girl was too much. He was having a good time just being in her presence.

"I really am sorry, though," she said with a sheepish smile then buried her face in her hands. "Let me know how I can make it up to you."

"I'll think of something."

His phone started dinging with an incoming text, followed quickly by another, and he realized that he was late for dinner with Carmen. But staring at the beautiful girl sitting next to him, it was hard to get his feet to move.

"I just realized, I didn't catch your name. I'm Dante Guzman."

"Ruby. Ruby Rhodes."

His phone dinged again, and she smiled wistfully. "Someone's trying to get a hold of you."

"Yeah," he said, suppressing a sigh. Reluctantly, he stood up and pulled his wallet from his pocket. Carmen's mouth on his cock would have to be his consolation prize.

He counted out enough money to cover their tab and leave a generous tip then threw it on the bar before turning back to her. "Well, Ruby Rhodes, I thoroughly enjoyed spending time with you, but I'm late for dinner."

"It was nice meeting you, too, Dante Guzman. Thank you for the drinks. Again, I'm sorry about your pants and the way I…" She blushed again.

He was about to turn and walk away—the last thing he wanted to do since it would most certainly mean he'd never see her again. He couldn't let that happen. Not yet. He wanted to spend more time with her. At least kiss her. Although he doubted he'd be satisfied with just kissing her.

"I just figured out how you can make it up to me."

She cocked her head. "How?"

"Have dinner with me tomorrow night."

"Tomorrow? Um…" she glanced around as if the bar walls could offer advice then looked back at him. "Sure, I guess."

"Where are you staying? I'll send a car for you at six."

She pulled her bottom lip between her teeth and stared at him like she was debating about something. Finally, she said, "How about if I meet you at the restaurant?"

He didn't like that idea one bit. It meant she could possibly stand him up.

"Are you sure? It's no problem for me to send a car."

"Dante, I'm a Texas girl. My daddy raised me to be adventurous not foolish. I'm a twenty-eight year old woman in a foreign country and just met you in a bar. I don't know anything about you other than you have excellent taste in whiskey and watches. It would be foolish to let you whisk me off in a car when I barely know you."

"I wish I could stay longer, so we could get to know each other better."

She stared into his eyes and softly murmured, "Me too."

"I look forward to tomorrow," he replied wistfully.

Goddammit, he didn't want to leave yet. But he'd have to take comfort knowing he'd secured a date with her tomorrow. It was time to go. After deciding on a place she could meet him for dinner, he turned and walked out. Carmen's mouth awaited.

Chapter Two

Ruby/a.k.a. Special Agent Kennedy Jones
Well, it was a start. She'd gotten a date for tomorrow—that was good. When he'd turned to leave without showing any interest, she'd been worried.

The profiler who'd studied Dante had told her she needed to play a little hard to get—that he liked the chase. But not too hard because he also liked being in control. If she came off too easy, she'd be lumped in with the masses—fucked and discarded. She needed to stand out from the women he usually dated. But if she was too prudish, she'd be written off. She had to come up with the balance that made him find her interesting enough to want to spend more time with her but also maintain some semblance of being demure, so he didn't see her as a threat.

She must have found a good blend. Although he hadn't quite responded the way she thought he would with the whole naively rubbing his dick over his pants bit. She'd opened the door for so much innuendo and flirting, and he barely peeked his head around the corner. Even after she lobbed in a few more softballs, he didn't take the bait.

She'd genuinely thought he wasn't interested and was wondering what she'd done wrong, then he at least asked her to dinner, so all was not lost.

Intel had suggested she was exactly his type—part of the reason she'd initially been considered for this assignment.

She'd hired a second trainer, worked out twice a day, and dieted even more than usual for the last six months. She'd even gotten a little Botox just to make sure she passed for twenty-eight. None of the women he'd dated in the past two years were older than thirty, and Kennedy was actually closer to forty than thirty.

The pictures in Dante's file did not do the man justice. He was panty-meltingly handsome with his strong, square jaw and perfect amount of grey in his jet-black hair—Ruby had known that. But up close, she could see his chocolate brown eyes had flecks of gold that twinkled like he had a secret. She'd even caught sight of a dimple. In all the photos in his file, he always looked so serious. He was tall, and his impeccably tailored suit fit his muscular body just right, but she wasn't prepared for what a commanding presence he emanated in real life.

This mission wasn't going to be a hardship, that was for sure. At least not until the end. Although she was nervous about when he took her to bed. The report read he "had dominant tendencies and liked his sexual partners to be submissive." She'd never had a dominant lover before.

Fortunately, her moral compass wasn't going to deter her from completing the assignment, something the agency already knew from when they originally profiled her and probably why she'd already gotten some of the missions she'd had. Having to fuck a mark wasn't a deal breaker. That, along with the many skills she'd acquired in the Marine Corps and continued to hone, had helped her become one of the most sought after undercover agents in the CIA.

Ruby Rhodes, rich girl oil-heiress, sent to Mexico by her father to learn Spanish was her cover. She was fluent in the language, but pretending not to understand gave her an advantage. People tended to talk more freely in front of you if they thought you didn't know what they were saying.

She took her time finishing her drink as she rehashed what had gone right and if there was anything she should have done differently. When she'd finished the expensive whiskey, she slid off the stool and retrieved the bags from the chair next to her. She'd had fun spending the CIA's money this afternoon on presents for her sister and mom, but she'd gone overboard in her attempt to seem like a rich girl. No matter, she'd donate the rest of her purchases.

Pulling her cell out of her oversized bag, she dialed the hotel's number for a ride as she walked across the dusty oak floor toward the old bar's pockmarked wooden door. She'd first thought it was a mistake when she'd walked in the dive bar. How could *this* be Dante Guzman's favorite place to stop for a drink? But there he'd been, sitting at the bar—just like surveillance had said he would be.

The luxury accommodations awaiting her back at her hotel was another perk to this assignment, and she was going to take full advantage of the oversized tub in her enormous bathroom after ordering room service.

Hey, I need to play the part if I'm going to be believable, she justified.

Drinking a seventy-five dollar shot had gone against everything her little trailer park existence had taught her. She knew it was going to be expensive if that was Dante's drink of choice, she just hadn't realized it would be that much in an old bar in Ensenada. To quell the inner trailer park little girl, she'd ordered a double.

It was as delicious as it had been when she drank it during her prep work to meet the cartel moneyman.

She tucked her phone in her purse as she stepped out into the warm summer night—closing her eyes to enjoy the summer breeze, only opening them when she ran smack dab into a tall, broad body who let out an "Oomph" when her body barreled into his.

"Oh, *discúlpame,*" she said automatically, then cringed. Not exactly the reaction of a woman just learning Spanish.

The man's face came into view wearing a knowing grin. "Miss Rhodes."

Shit. She went on the offensive before he even had a chance to ask her about her Spanish.

"Oh, Dante! It's you! I swear I'm not trying to harm you on purpose," she said with a laugh that was way too high pitched, even to her own ears. "Even though I'm sure it looks that way, all the bumbling I've done around you." *Breathe, Keni.*

Wait, what is he doing here?

In a more subdued voice, she cocked her head and asked, "Did you forget something?"

His hand went to her hip, where his thumb subtly stroked the material of her white designer dress. "My dinner plans changed, so I thought I'd come back and see if you'd like to join me."

Except he said it in Spanish.

She blinked at him rapidly then said with a placating smile, "I'm sorry, I have no idea what you just said to me."

His grin was crooked when he asked—in English this time, "Are you sure? You seemed to know some Spanish just a minute ago."

"Positive. But that's why I'm here. To learn. I overheard the bellman at the hotel say *discúlpame* earlier when he ran into someone, so I just put two and two together. Did I say it right?"

He eyed her suspiciously for a beat then a slow grin formed on his face as it relaxed. "Yes, you said it right. So, would you like to have dinner with me?"

"I thought you already had dinner plans?"

"I cancelled them. I didn't think it'd be fair to my companion to be thinking about you all evening when I should be paying attention to her."

Her stomach dipped at his admission. Genuinely.

It's just because that means the mission is going better than planned, she reasoned. It had nothing to do with the fact that she had found herself honestly enjoying his company earlier.

"Oh. Well, what if I say I'm busy?" she teased, batting her eyelashes coyly at him.

He gave her a grin that melted her panties while he leaned closer, wrapping a strand of her hair around his finger as he murmured, "Aw, don't do that, little one. Then I'll have to eat alone and go to bed hungry."

She caught the slip although she knew perfectly well it was anything but a slip. He didn't say *or* go to bed hungry—he said *and*.

"What are you implying? If I have dinner with you, you'll go to bed satisfied?"

His eyes flashed lustfully at her under the orange street lights, but he shrugged noncommittally. "More so than I would if I were to eat alone." He slowly withdrew his finger, leaving a perfect ringlet on her shoulder, then stared into her eyes. "Who knows, maybe I'll even have dessert. Do you like dessert, Ruby?"

How strong he was coming onto her now made her immediately suspicious. She'd practically sat on his lap inside the bar trying to get this type of reaction, but he'd not taken her up on it. What had changed?

One goddamn word. *Discúlpame.*

Fuck. She needed to do some damage control. Except she wasn't exactly certain what that should look like. Did she play hard to get or take him up on his offer? What was the best strategy, long term?

It must have been the Macallan talking because she heard herself purring, "I love dessert." Then leaned her tits against his arm. "What's your favorite?"

Guess I'm going with the sex strategy.

He stared down at her with his gaze focused on her mouth. "Strawberry shortcake," then moved up to her eyes. "Yours?"

With her eyes deadlocked on his, she replied in a low, sultry voice, "Mexican swizzle sticks."

The corner of his mouth turned up. "I happen to know the perfect place you can get those."

"What a lucky coincidence for me to have sat next to you at the bar."

"Serendipity, indeed."

There was a hint of sarcasm in his voice, putting her on edge. Something told her he wasn't buying her story. She was going to have to turn on the charm and make him believe it.

****

Dante

He knew damn well luck had absolutely nothing to do with her sitting next to him tonight.

Walking out of the bar earlier with a smile, he'd been replaying the evening's events in his mind when it hit him out of nowhere. If he was going to design his ideal woman—she would be it. And she just so happened to be at his favorite bar the same time he was, ordered the same drink as him, and proceeded to flirt with him? Something wasn't adding up. This was too good to be true. Not that women didn't come onto him... they did. All the time, actually. Money and power were like female catnip, and he had plenty of both. But this chick... She'd been *too* perfect.

Dante was on the phone with one of his investigators in the States the second he was seated in the back of his waiting car.

"Find out what you can about a Ruby Rhodes out of Texas, twenty-eight years old, and get back to me ASAP."

He then called John, his best friend and second-in-command, and asked him to do the same. Even though John was currently in South America working on securing connections for when the Guzmans expanded, he was much faster in replying—calling him back before Dante had even reached the restaurant where Carmen was waiting for him.

"This is what I've found out. She exists—at least on paper."

"What the fuck does that mean?" Dante snarled.

"It means, there's a paper trail for her—education, credit cards, social media presence... and they're all dated appropriately, so if you were doing a superficial search, it'd pass the smell test. But, when I started digging—really digging, everything about her has been established in the last eight to nine months. Even accounts that are supposed to be ten years old were really only created recently. Someone has gone to a lot of trouble to make it look like she has a much longer history than she really does."

Dante sighed. "I knew she was too perfect."

John continued. "My best guess is CIA. Whoever created her identity was no slouch. They did a damn good job. She has a credit score in her name, a degree... hell, there's even a lease to a penthouse in Houston in her name that I'm sure is really where someone is putting up his mistress."

"Get in touch with our guy on the inside and find out how much it's going to cost me to get her real name and what she's doing here."

"That's going to take some time," John warned.

"That's okay," Dante grinned devilishly "I'm going to have a little fun in the meantime. Hey, if I call you back later and am talking bullshit—just go along, okay?"

He instructed his driver to take him back to the bar then dialed Carmen directly.

Her voice was husky when she answered, "Hello there."

"I'm sorry, gorgeous. Work is keeping me busy tonight, so I'm not going to be able make it after all. But please, have dinner on me. And make sure to order the most expensive bottle of wine."

The dark-haired woman on the other end laughed. "I already did. I'm sorry you can't break away. I was looking forward to your company tonight."

"Perhaps another time."

"I look forward to it."

He clicked off and began planning all the things he was going to do to that little redhead CIA agent's mouth, and how she'd willingly let him if he was her target. And how satisfying it was going to be knowing it wasn't because she really wanted to. He just hoped she was still there.

He pulled up to the bar and got out before his driver could open his door. Marching to the door, he had just reached it when it opened up and a flash of red hair barreled straight into him. A sweet voice gasped, "*Discúlpame.*"

His hand steadied the offender running into him, but he already knew who it was. He glanced down and noticed the cute freckles across her nose, her green eyes widened momentarily when she realized she'd said *excuse me*, in the right context, in Spanish.

No hablo my ass.

She'd then agreed to ride with him to dinner, probably in an effort to distract him from his suspicions, which he dangled out in front of her knowing she'd worry and try to appease him—and he was planning on taking full advantage of that. Maybe that made him a bastard, but this chick wasn't exactly being on the level with him, so he was going to have no remorse when he was balls deep in her pussy in about an hour, ninety minutes tops, then kicked her ass to the curb when he was through with her.

The CIA could suck his balls.

Dante let out a small chuckle. They were going to—literally.

"What's so funny?" she asked from the seat next to him in the back of his car.

"Just what a coincidence it was that you were at the bar at the same time I was. I mean what are the odds? Not to mention you like Mexican swizzle sticks."

He was baiting her, and she took it hook, line, and sinker.

Brushing her tits against his biceps, she squeezed his inner thigh and whispered in his ear, "And you like strawberry shortcake."

That was all the invitation Dante needed, and he grabbed a fistful of hair at the back of her head, holding her in place as his mouth plundered hers. She responded immediately, her arms at his shoulders, holding on for dear life as she returned the intensity of his kiss.

His hand slid under her dress, inching up her thigh until he could feel the heat emanating from her pussy. Rubbing circles over her panties, he growled in her ear, "I think I want dessert first."

Ruby let out a submissive whimper and subtly opened her legs wider, and he couldn't help but grin.

"Mmm, good girl. Spread those legs for me."

The fabric between her legs was getting damp, and Dante pushed it to the side and plunged one finger deep inside her pussy, moving it in and out.

"Look how fucking wet you are!" he exclaimed then slowly pulled out and dragged his fingertip up and down her slit, spreading her juices along her folds. Finding her clit, he began to wiggle his finger rapidly over it, only pausing to dip his finger inside her again for more natural lubricant.

"When was the last time you were fucked? Your pussy is so tight."

She gasped as he smeared more of her juices before resuming his manipulation of her hard nub.

He felt her start to tense up and growled as he increased the tempo, "That's it, little slut. Come on my fucking hand."

And fucking come she did.

She began to chant, "Oh my god, oh my god," as she gripped his biceps tight. Her body was as taut as a wire—this girl must've needed this more than he did. Letting out a long, low moan she arched back with her eyes closed and her mouth in the form of an 'Oh' right before she began to shudder and jerk. Watching her come undone at his hand was the most erotic thing he'd witnessed in a long time, and his dick was hard as fucking steel.

He didn't let up until she squeezed her thighs together and opened her eyes, looking over at him with a sheepish smile.

Dante didn't return the smile. His gaze intense when he leaned down and enunciated in her ear, "Suck my cock, bitch."

Chapter Three

Ruby

His words were crude, meant to debase her. Yet, she'd never been more turned in on in her life. Apparently, she had a submissive side—for real... who knew?

Not her. She was a kickass CIA assassin. Submission in her real life was a foreign concept, but she was getting her rocks off playing the part of a submissive right now. It probably helped that she hadn't had sex with anyone other than her vibrator in almost a year. And Dante's dominance was hot as fuck. And that orgasm he'd just given her... holy shit.

She obediently slid between his legs and began unbuckling his belt as he clicked the intercom to the driver with a simple order of "Drive around." Yeah, like *that* wasn't obvious they were fooling around in the backseat.

He lifted his ass when she began to tug on his trousers, his gorgeous cock bouncing when she pulled his boxer briefs down along with his pants, leaving them pooled at his ankles.

Ruby stroked his shaft reverently while getting acquainted with it. As far as cocks went, his was practically perfect. Straight as an arrow, above average length and girth but not so much that she couldn't handle it, and she rubbed her face against the velvety smooth surface with her eyes closed as she took in his masculine scent.

Dante grabbed a fistful of her hair and steered her mouth to his balls, and she compliantly began to run her tongue along the outline of his sac before sucking one in.

"Take them both," he directed, and once again, she did as he instructed without question, stuffing her mouth full of Dante's balls while trying to massage them with her tongue.

With a loud *slurp!* Ruby popped them out of her mouth and hesitated, waiting for his next command. Using her hair as a handle, he guided her mouth to his cock, and she dutifully took him as deep as she could, causing him to let out a slight gasp.

Getting his shaft nice and slippery, she began to stroke him from the base as she bobbed her head up and down.

"That's it. Fuuuck, yeah."

She took him deep again, and he held her head in place and thrust up, causing her eyes to water.

"Get ready to swallow, slut."

Kennedy was more of a spitter than a swallower, but apparently her alter-ego, Ruby was about to embrace it because she didn't even hesitate. Slurping off his cock, she took him shallow in her mouth; moaning around his shaft and jerking him fast until she tasted the saltiness of cum hit the tip of her tongue and then swallowed, looking up at him as she did. He closed his eyes and groaned, throwing his head back like the sight of her was more than he could handle.

She felt like a goddamn porn star. It was empowering as fuck.

Popping his cock out of her mouth, she ran her hands along his inner thigh as she remained between his legs, gazing up at him like a good little submissive. Dante opened his eyes and looked down at her with a soft smile, caressing her cheek before moving his thumb to her bottom lip as he stared at her mouth.

"Such a pretty mouth," he murmured, pulling her bottom lip down and rubbing it hard—like he was smearing her lipstick, then moved back to stroking the side of her face tenderly. "Such a beautiful face. Next time I'm going to paint it with my cum."

Dante tugged on her biceps to move her back to the seat next to him and spread her legs apart. He slid one hand under her dress and pushed her panties between her nether lips and into her pussy. His other hand held her chin firmly, and he growled with his lips against her ear, "Then I'm going to fuck your pussy hard and come again when I'm balls deep inside you. And you're going to thank me for it by cleaning my cock with your mouth." He pressed his fingers in her, pushing the fabric deeper. "If you do a good job and beg me, I might let you come again."

His words and his manhandling of her had her wet.

He released her chin but slid his hand around her throat, squeezing only slightly as if to convey the power of his position.

"Do you think you'd like that, slut?"

"Yes," Ruby whispered as if saying it out loud was a confessional.

He squeezed harder. "Yes, what?"

"Yes, sir."

Dante fucked her shallow with his fingers, her panties still shoved inside her pussy creating a barrier.

She let out a frustrated moan and was met with a hard slap to her clit over the fabric. Followed by a succession of swats to her center.

"You've soaked your panties."

Her underwear was drenched, she could feel it. She wanted nothing more than for him to slide them to the side again and pressed against his palm hoping to convey just that.

He chuckled as he removed his hand and pulled up his pants, put his cock inside his underwear, and zipped up. He was done playing with her. After he had tucked his shirt in and buckled his belt, he clicked the intercom to the driver. "Take us to the restaurant."

That's it?

Ruby tried to act unaffected when she pulled a brush from her bag and ran it through her long, red hair, then took a compact out to look at herself as she reapplied her makeup. Good as new; no one would be able to tell she'd just been used like a slut and had her face fucked in the back of a limo. But her underwear sticking to her pussy served as a reminder that she had and of just how much she'd loved it.

She hadn't meant to fuck him already—he'd just made it impossible not to. Now she needed to turn on the charm because she might be in danger of becoming a one-night stand, and that would be difficult to explain to the agency.

****

Dante

Damn, he'd enjoyed using her in the car. He hadn't planned on fucking her so soon, but the way she looked up at him with those innocent green eyes and that pouty mouth, when he knew she was anything but innocent... he hadn't been able to help himself. Plus, he'd wanted to check her for weapons.

Her little submissive whimpers at his manhandling of her brought his dom out in full force. He'd originally been planning on fucking her once and shoving her out the door with cum all over her face. But when he described what he wanted to do to her later, her pussy became drenched. That had to be explored—at least for the night. He could kick her out in the morning.

They walked into one of his favorite restaurants in Ensenada. Well, he walked in—she strutted like she was used to being the center of attention. Tonight was no exception— all eyes were on her when they were shown to their table—a corner booth, and she situated herself next to him.

He already knew what he wanted to order, so he didn't need to look at the menu and instead was able to subtly stare at her tits, the pale mounds of flesh peeking out between the buttons of her blouse drove him crazy.

She glanced at him out of the corner of her eye and smiled as her hand discreetly began rubbing his inner thigh.

When she set her menu down, he asked, "Did you decide?"

"I did. I think I'll have the filet."

"How do you usually like it prepared?"

She tilted her head, confused why he'd care. "Medium?"

"Good. I'll order for you. Go to the restroom and take off your panties. Bring them back to me."

"What?"

"Did you not understand me? I'm fairly certain I was speaking English. Give. Me. Your. Panties. Maybe you'll understand Spanish. *Dame tus bragas.*"

"But..."

He cut her off. "Or you can take them off here at the table. Either is fine." His expression let her know it wasn't up for debate.

Still, she challenged him. "Why should I?"

Raising his water glass to his lips, he smirked. "Because you want to."

She stared at him with her mouth slightly open. He set the glass on the table and pulled her closer, his hand at the nape of her neck as he leaned his lips to her ear with a warm smile. To an outsider, it looked like a gesture of affection, but his hand gripped her hair as he growled, "Don't act like you don't enjoy doing what you're told, little slut. If I ordered you to suck my cock under the table, you'd do it."

"No I wouldn't," she whispered defiantly, but he could see her chest rising.

"But you're imagining what that would be like. Sucking my cock anytime I told you to. Spreading your legs when I snap my fingers. Being used like a little fuck doll. And I'm just the man to use you." Dante discreetly pinched her nipple. "Now go take those fucking panties off. You know they're soaked again. I can smell how wet you are."

She let out a little gasp and moved to slide out of the booth when he put his hand on her wrist. "And no one touches that pussy but me. That includes you. Got it?"

"Yes, sir."

His cock jumped at her use of the word *sir*, and he stared at her ass as she sashayed toward the bathroom—he knew the extra sway in her hips was for his benefit. Everything about her story might be bullshit, but she was a natural submissive. He wondered if that's why she was given this assignment— his bedroom preferences weren't exactly a secret. If he had to guess, her red hair and hot body had been the initial reason; the fact that she liked being used probably wasn't as well known. The CIA probably thought that could be faked, which it probably could... to an extent. But her body's response had been no act.

She definitely was going to enjoy what he was going to do to her later. And so was he. Just thinking about it had him hard. She arrived back at the table and slipped her balled up panties into his palm while refusing to look at his face. He closed his hand into a fist and brought it to his nose to take a theatrical deep breath in, closing his eyes as he did.

"Your ode de pussy is spectacular."

Her cheeks blushed at his crudeness, but what was she going to do? Blow her assignment and walk out? No, and he was going to take full advantage of that fact as he explored this side of her. He wondered if she had even known this about herself. Was she ashamed to like it so much?

God, he fucking hoped so. Would serve the conniving bitch right.

Then she smiled at him, her green eyes tender, and she attempted to have a normal conversation with him, like they'd had at the bar. She was a fucking pro because he soon found himself laughing and hanging on her every word, wanting to know more about her... the *real* her. He was enjoying himself so much, he'd even take the bullshit persona if it meant more of this.

And that realization instantly pissed him off. Why couldn't she be real?

His conflicted feelings only fueled his desire to punish her later. He kept reminding himself that he was onto her, that *he* was the one playing *her*. And yet, when she started laughing at her own joke as they waited for the check, he couldn't help but lean down and kiss her gently on the mouth. The soft moan that escaped her lips when she returned the kiss sure as fuck felt real.

Chapter Four

Ruby

Back inside the limo, Dante pulled her onto his lap and traced his hand up her inner thigh. His touch was feather light as his fingers skimmed her bare pussy, then down her other thigh. As he spoke on the phone in Spanish, he did this repeatedly, making her want to push her hips down, so he would touch her.

"What do you mean the shipment's been postponed?" Pause. "Okay, yeah. So how delayed are we talking?" Pause. "Enrique is not going to like it but okay. I'll call him first thing in the morning."

She knew he was talking about Enrique Guzman, *El Jefe*—the head of the Guzman cartel, his uncle, and her true target. Enrique's power in Mexico was growing exponentially, along with his brutality and brazenness, and he was becoming a thorn in the CIA's side with his refusal to play nice with others. Her orders were to infiltrate the cartel by any means necessary and kill Enrique. After studying the Guzman family, Dante Guzman seemed her best way in. Dante was the moneyman of the cartel and would have regular contact with Enrique although recent word on the street was the two men had been butting heads lately about the direction the organization was going. That might alter the original timetable a little.

Dante's jaw was clenched tight when he disconnected the call, and she tried to quell his bad mood by kissing his neck and playing with the hair above his collar. She genuinely was feeling the need to soothe him.

"Thank you for dinner. I enjoyed your company." With her lips still on his skin, she murmured, "You are a brilliant man, and I love talking to you."

That wasn't bullshit. He was fucking brilliant. Stanford MBA smart, to be exact, and he spoke five languages—both things she knew only from studying his file; he hadn't shared any of that with her yet. He'd been engaged and interesting in their conversations, but he hadn't talked a lot about himself personally. Other than her bullshit back story, her dialogue with him had been genuine.

His fingers continued their torment under her skirt.

"Normally I like to stay at a hotel when I'm *entertaining*, but my favorite place is booked tonight. Would you like to accompany me to my estate? Before you answer, you should know, you won't be leaving until tomorrow. I mean, you'd be free to actually *leave* anytime you wanted, but no one on my staff will be available to drive you anywhere."

"I guess I could get a cab."

"Maybe. Except all the reputable cab companies stop running at midnight during the week. You'd be rolling the dice on who picked you up."

"Maybe the hotel would send a shuttle."

"I suppose there's that possibility. If you want it."

Why was she arguing about this? It wasn't like she was actually going to leave—he was inviting her into his home for fuck's sake! Getting inside his house tonight put her three weeks ahead of schedule.

Shit, she wished she'd known things were going to go so well. She'd left the bugging equipment in her hotel room, never thinking it a possibility he'd take her home. Of course, she hadn't planned on having an orgasm with him either, and apparently there was at least another one promised in her future tonight. Granted, she'd been told she'd have to beg for it, but looking at his beautiful face, that wasn't something she was exactly opposed to. Just the opposite, if she were being honest.

All in the name of the assignment.

He interrupted her thoughts by pinching her nipple with his free hand as he continued the slow tease of her pussy. "So, is that a yes, you'd like to join me? Or should I have the driver drop you at your hotel?"

"I would love to join you, but do you mind if we stop off at my hotel, so I can drop my packages off, get my toothbrush and a change of clothes for tomorrow?"

"Yes, I do mind." He began to stroke her slit, which was drenched. "Your packages will be fine in the car, I have plenty of extra toothbrushes, and I'll send someone out in the morning to get you a new outfit, so you aren't doing the walk of shame, arriving back at your hotel in what you're currently wearing."

"I would only be a minute," she argued. She really should get the bugging equipment... but his fingers were making it hard to care about that. Which was really unprofessional of her and so not like her.

He plunged a finger in her pussy, and she let out a small moan.

"No." It was one word, but the tone let her know it was not up for discussion.

She thought about insisting he let her get her things, but then worried he'd just leave her at the hotel—and she definitely didn't want that. She was getting a chance to check out the interior of his house. Then there was the other thing she was looking forward to—whether or not Dante would make good on his earlier threat about what he was going to do to her.

She hadn't yet had a chance to analyze just why her body had reacted like he was its rightful owner—and maybe that was for the better. Getting into her own head right now could compromise everything.

They drove a few miles out of town until they reached well lit, ornate iron gates and a twelve- foot high brick fence that seemed to stretch for a mile in either direction. Guards with large guns strapped to their centers stepped outside the guardhouse to briefly inspect the car. The gates opened, and they waved the car through.

She was about to quip about him being paranoid—since he hadn't exactly shared with her at dinner that he was a high-ranking cartel member, she would be expected to question such high security. But then she caught sight of the grounds and caught her breath.

Every magazine that she'd ever read, every show she'd seen on TV, every movie... nothing prepared her for what she was witnessing in real life. Pictures of the meticulously manicured hedges and grass had not been in his file. And that was only what she could see illuminated by the outdoor lighting. Ruby could only imagine how spectacular it had to be during the day.

"Your grounds are stunning," she murmured, trying to sound impressed but not too impressed. She was supposed to be an heiress, after all, so meticulous lawns should be second nature to her, but she also wanted to let him know that she appreciated how beautiful they were.

"Thank you. I do take great pride in them."

The long, winding paved driveway turned into cobblestone, and they pulled up to a Mediterranean-style estate with a large, circular center turret housing an oversized front door and smaller, matching round turrets on each end of the house. A mission tile roof completed the Mediterranean look. It was elegant and tasteful—exactly like the photos in the CIA's dossier of him.

They got out of the car, and Dante held her elbow as he escorted her inside.

A large chandelier lit a modern entry with warm, rich colors and dark wood. The large arrangement of fresh flowers on the foyer table gave the place a homey, welcoming vibe, and Ruby instantly felt comfortable.

"Wow, this is beautiful, Dante," she uttered as she looked around at the tall walls adorned with artwork and the high, ornate, dome ceiling.

"Thank you," he said dismissively like he'd heard it before. "My bedroom is on the second floor, this way," and he ushered her toward the curved, wooden staircase.

"You're not going to give me a tour?"

He pulled his neck back and looked at her suspiciously, like she'd made an odd request. "No."

"Oh."

It was silly, but out of everything he'd done tonight—*that* was the one thing that made her feel cheap. And it wasn't just because she had ulterior motives for wanting to see the house. She felt like the only thing he thought she was worthy of seeing was his bedroom because that's where he was going to fuck her.

He must have sensed that she felt put out and let out a long sigh. "Forgive me. I don't usually have visitors in my home without planning and preparation. I'm very particular about who is allowed here and when. I'll show you around in the morning."

"Thank you. I guess I'm flattered you invited me in the first place."

"Yes, well..." Leaving the thought unfinished, Dante tugged on her hand, and they started walking up the stairs.

"Besides, if my housekeeper knows I have a guest, she'll feel compelled to come out and cook something. Poor Rosa is probably already in her nightgown—you wouldn't want to disturb a sweet old lady's rest, would you?"

"Well, when you put it that way." She couldn't help but giggle.

And just like that, she liked him again and was nervously excited about what he had promised was going to happen.

As it turned out, he hadn't been bluffing.

He closed the heavy, wooden door to his bedroom and locked it behind them. Then with a low, menacing voice said, "Take off your clothes and get on your fucking knees."

She walked into the middle of the room, taking in his masculine furniture and décor under the low lighting, while slowly unzipping her dress as he'd instructed. She turned around to look at him, finding him staring at her intently. Ruby let the front drop to her waist and shimmied out of the material.

"Leave the heels on," he ordered gruffly.

Keeping eye contact with him, she reached around and unclasped her bra, letting the straps fall down her arms as her breasts were exposed. Dante's nostrils flared while his gaze fell to her bare boobs and stalked toward her, unfastening his belt as he did.

He circled her, looking her up and down, as if he were evaluating her like she was a piece of art he was deciding whether or not he wanted to bid on. She was comfortable with her body—she knew she looked good. Still it was unnerving to have him assess her like he was doing, all without saying a word. Seeing the bulge in his pants helped reassure her though.

Finally, he murmured from her backside, "So perfect," then wrapped one hand around her waist and another around her throat as he came up behind her. The power he exerted over her was such a turn on. Probably because she wasn't really afraid that he'd hurt her.

"Are you already wet for me, *Ruby*?" he whispered in her ear before reaching between her legs to answer his own question. He chuckled deviously when he found her wet and plunged one finger inside her. "Such a good slut."

She let out a whimper but didn't dare respond with his hand still around her neck.

He ran his lips down her face as he spoke. "Do you remember what I told you is going to happen next?"

She nodded with another whimper of, "Mmm hmm."

Dante nipped at her ear. "What? Tell me."

"You're going to fuck my face then come all over it." Her voice was barely a whisper.

He pressed into her pussy harder. "Oh, you like that idea. Your pussy just gushed."

The truth was, she did like it. Playing the part of his submissive was no hardship.

"Then what am I going to do?"

"Fuck me."

His fingers moved in and out of her. "Not before you clean my cock off with your mouth. *How* am I going to fuck you?"

"Hard... and deep."

"Balls deep," he corrected. "And then what is going to happen?"

"You're going to come again in my pussy."

Frankly, she wasn't sure she was a believer he'd be able to recover very quickly, let alone come again. He was thirty-nine years old, after all, and had already come once tonight.

He moved his fingers from inside her pussy to her clit and tightened his grip around her neck, ever so slightly. "And if you're a good little slut, then what?"

"I can come too."

She wanted to come *now*.

"But only if you..."

"Beg." She blurted out in a whisper, her orgasm creeping closer.

"Do you think you'll like begging me, sweet *Ruby*?"

"Yes."

Dante stilled his hand, and she wanted to cry. "Yes, what?"

"Yes, sir," she panted, hoping that would spur his hand to move again.

Good," he said harshly, then gave her clit four fast slaps. "Get on your fucking knees."

She should have known better than to doubt his ability to perform.

After coming all over her face, as promised, he smeared his seed around with his cock then tugged on her hair for her to open her mouth and clean him off.

"That's it," he moaned with his eyes closed, his hand on the back of her head.

He pulled out, his smile wistful when he looked down at her and traced his thumb along the corner of her mouth. "So beautiful." He stared at her cum-covered face for a few beats, as if admiring his handiwork then whispered, "I'll be right back," and walked toward what she assumed was his bathroom en suite. She remained on her knees with her eyes lowered, still in her heels until he disappeared, then her eyes quickly darted around the room, making a mental note of where she could plant bugs the next time she was there.

If there was a next time.

Ruby needed to give a porn star performance to ensure that happened, which wasn't asking much of her. She was soaked, she had been so turned on being used by him.

He came back in the room with a hand towel and gently cleaned her off, studying her face as he did. "So fucking perfect..." He'd said it with affection, but there was something ominous in his eyes as he uttered the words. Then he grabbed a fistful of her hair and tugged with one hand while helping her to her feet by her arm with the other. His hand under her chin, he whispered in her ear through gritted teeth, "On the fucking bed," then walked her to the king size, four poster bed, his hand around her neck, before bending her over with one hard smack to the ass as he did.

Even though he'd already given her the night's itinerary, she was still wet with anticipation over what was about to transpire. His manhandling of her just intensified her excitement.

The weight of his body was on her back, and he murmured, "I just got tested, and I'm clean. Are you on the pill? Because I want to fuck you raw."

He waited for her to answer, and for a split second she almost lied because the idea of no barrier between them was appealing. Finally, she whispered, "I'm not on birth control." He nodded and reached into his nightstand, producing a square package. The condom was on in seconds, and he dug his fingers into her hips, slamming into her balls deep, just like he promised.

Although he was fucking her deep, after the initial thrust, it wasn't hard, and his tempo was slow and steady.

"Your pussy feels so good, I could fuck you all night."

His cock felt so good, she'd happily let him.

He reached in front of her and began toying with her clit.

"Do you want to come?" he taunted.

With her mouth slightly agape from panting, she nodded her head and squeaked out, "Yes, sir."

"Beg me. Beg me to let you come."

"Please, sir, may I come?"

"No," he snarled but didn't let up on his ministrations of her clit as he moved in and out of her pussy. She felt her body flush, and she clenched her stomach, trying not to orgasm.

"Please, sir. Please. I'll do anything. Please let me come."

His chuckle was low and deep. "Come, you naughty slut. Come on my dick."

That was all she needed to push her over the edge, her climax overloading her senses to the point it felt like she could feel every neuron in her body firing as she cried out in ecstasy.

Dante held her hips and thrust into her hard and fast, roaring his release moments later. The primal power of it was intoxicating, and another orgasm shuddered through her before the last one had even subsided.

He dropped onto her back, panting, and pinning her under him. She could feel his emotions emanating through his body onto hers. He began to tenderly kiss the back of her neck, whispering sweet words of adoration in Spanish as his hands ran down her sides. It was a complete one eighty from the domineering, debasement of her he'd just done— treatment she'd loved, and yet, this also felt right.

He disappeared, she assumed to dispose of the condom and was back in seconds. Ruby let him wrap his arms around her and pull her under the covers, trying not to think about how he was nothing but a mark because right now, she loved being in his arms. If she let herself be reminded this wasn't real, she knew her body would betray her, and she'd want to pull away from his embrace.

"Oh, *Bella...*" Dante murmured with his lips against her hair. "What am I going to do about you?"

****

Dante

Until he was certain Ruby hadn't been sent to kill him, there was no way he would be able to sleep in her presence. Although watching the soft rise and fall of her chest while she drifted off had a lulling effect, and he situated himself with one arm wrapped around her middle, her body pulled in tight next to his in a spooning position. If she stirred, he'd know it.

At least, that's what he'd thought. He woke up to the sun's morning rays, feeling content for the first time in a long time. The sex had been amazing, but so had her companionship. It was only after he laid there with a smile on his face rehashing last night's sexscapades that he realized he should not be alone in his bed.

But alone he was.

He sat up with a start. *So much for knowing if she moved.* He was considering himself lucky to not have had his throat slit, only to realize she could have wreaked havoc in other ways.

Shit, shit, shit.

He'd have to have his room swept for any electronic surveillance and check the cameras to see if she'd ventured out of his room.

Ruby reappeared wearing nothing but a towel around her middle while rubbing another towel on her wet auburn hair. She didn't have a stitch of makeup on, and her untamed hair was dripping onto her shoulders. She looked so damn sexy—perfect and pure, and his morning wood got even harder. Putting his arm around the back of his head, he leaned against the headboard and watched her.

"Good morning," she said with a smile when she noticed he was awake and looking at her. "I hope it's okay I borrowed your shower."

"Absolutely." His voice was raspy from sleep. "Next time, wake me up, and I'll join you."

She paused toweling her hair to look directly at him. "There's going to be a next time?"

He pulled his arm from behind his head and sat up straighter. "You tell me. I know my brand of sex isn't for everyone."

"Well," she looked down shyly and adjusted the towel around her body then glanced back up at him. "I, um, liked it."

Dante didn't know if it was her CIA persona talking or the real girl whose name he'd yet to learn. His gut told him it was the real girl who was a natural submissive—at least in bed. Out of the bedroom was another story.

His feet hit the floor at the same time, and he wasted no time stalking toward her. Her eyes were wide, but she stood her ground, not shriveling away, but not challenging him either when he untucked the towel covering her and discarded it to the floor, then cupped one creamy breast in each hand and backed her up until the backs of her knees hit the bed. She sat down with a thud, and he knelt between her legs, looking up at her while her pink middle beckoned him.

"I'm glad you liked it." He dipped his head and swiped up her slit with his tongue. "I loved it." He lapped at her folds and murmured, "And I love how you taste."

Ruby leaned back on her elbows and dropped her legs wide at the knees to accommodate his broad body, letting out little cooing sounds as he continued to lick her pussy. Her body was so responsive to his touch—it was sexy as fuck.

He twisted a finger inside her cunt, her walls wrapping firmly around his finger in a welcoming invitation, just like it had with his cock last night. Her pussy knew who it belonged to.

Flicking his tongue rapidly over her clit, he finger fucked her at the same time—then switched his fingers and tongue when he felt her begin to tense up.

"That's it, baby. Come on my tongue. Let me taste you," he murmured as he darted his tongue in and out of her tight pussy while polishing her clit faster with his fingers.

She let out little mewls and bucked her hips up, and Dante immediately put an arm around her stomach to hold her in place while he continued his attack between her legs. Her tiny nub was hard as he continued rubbing it fast—her breaths were shallower as her body became tauter. Until finally, she arched off the bed with a long, "Ohhhhh, god yes!" then began to thrash around him.

"Fuuuuck," he growled as her juices flooded his tongue. "You taste amazing."

He was still holding her tightly when she finally went still, her legs and arms limp, and he sucked her pussy lips between his teeth, tugging gently until she looked down at him.

"You're fucking beautiful, Ruby Rhodes."

Her eyes were still glassy when she reached down and cupped his cheek. "You're amazing, Dante Guzman."

He lifted himself off the floor and tweaked her nipple with a grin.

"Let me go grab a shower, then we'll go down for breakfast."

It was a gamble, leaving her alone in his room, but he'd already planned on having it swept for spying devices later. What else could she do in the five minutes it was going to take for him to shower?

Chapter Five

Dante

He'd had new clothes delivered to her, as promised, along with some strappy nude sandals with a kitten heel. It wasn't anything fancy, just a designer sundress with yellows and greens that would bring out her eyes and emphasize her auburn hair. He found it interesting how much he'd enjoyed picking it out and purchasing it for her.

"Wow," she uttered when she pulled it out of the bag and held it up next to her body as she looked in the mirror. "Kudos to your shopper. This is something I would have picked for myself."

"Actually, I selected it, and the shoes—from Maricella's online shop."

Her eyes narrowed even as a slow grin spread across her face. "*You* picked this? No, you didn't."

"I did. Last night on my phone while you were next to me snoring."

She gasped, and her jaw dropped in offense. "I don't snore!"

That made him chuckle, and he bopped her nose with the tip of his finger. "Yes, you do. Just a little. It was cute though. It made me want to kiss you. But I knew that would wake you, and I knew you needed to sleep since I'd worn you out."

She bit her bottom lip as if trying to disguise her grin and looked up at him. "You did wear me out. But in the best way possible."

God, she was fucking perfect. Gorgeous, intelligent, articulate, and his perfect sexual partner. It wasn't fucking fair that she wasn't real, and that pissed him off a little, but he tamped it down. After all, if he was planning on turning the tables on her and getting her to fall in love with *him*, then he needed to treat her like a princess—at least outside the bedroom. She'd already proven she liked his dirty mouth and how he dominated and used her sexually.

And fuck had he enjoyed manhandling her.

She dressed quickly and they went downstairs to have breakfast on the patio overlooking the grounds. He was proud of his estate—especially the expansive lawn and gardens, and found sitting outside looking at it while enjoying his morning coffee helped start his day off right. He had a feeling that having Ruby across from him was only going to amplify that.

How fucked up were the women he'd dated that he'd rather spend time with someone he knew to be a CIA operative sent to infiltrate his family's cartel and, quite possibly, kill him?

Keep your friends close and your enemies closer and all that, he guessed. At least that was going to be his justification for keeping her around awhile, anyway.

It had nothing to do with what her smile did to him.

Nothing.

Or how her emerald green eyes looked submissively up at him when his cock was in her mouth.

Turning the tables on her was going to be exactly what she deserved.

****

Ruby

They had a delicious breakfast on his patio—the two *abuelas* who were his fulltime housekeepers doted on him like he was their own son and looked on with curiosity at Ruby, smiling brightly at her as they poured coffee into Dante's fine china teacup and filled her juice glass.

Rosa spoke basic English, while Maria did not. Ruby kept having to catch herself from talking in Spanish to converse with Maria. She hated having to act like she didn't understand the woman who seemed eager to communicate with her. Instead, she put on her best 'learning the language' act and spoke in crude, short sentences to get her point across and waited patiently until Dante translated what the woman replied.

After their breakfast dishes were cleared away, Dante stood and reached for her hand. "I promised you a tour. Do you want to start with the grounds or inside?"

"It's such a beautiful morning, let's start outside."

Conversation with the gorgeous Mexican flowed easily, and any silence between them was comfortable. He asked her about her background, which fortunately her cover story had been drilled into her, so her responses were quick with no hesitation.

"How long have you been in Ensenada?"

"Just a few days."

"I'm not detecting an accent that you Texans are famous for."

She was ready for this question. "I lost mine at the age of ten when my daddy sent me to boarding school up North with the Yankees. I never got it back, even when I came back to Texas for college."

"So, are you planning on doing good things here in Mexico?"

"As opposed to bad things?" she giggled. Kennedy, as a rule, did not giggle. Perfecting the art in preparation for her role as Ruby had taken a good deal of time. It wasn't exactly a trait she admired in her alter ego and had to consciously do it.

The corner of his mouth lifted. "Well, bad things can be good if done right."

"So you've shown me."

"So, why Spanish? And why Ensenada?"

"I live in the US, learning Spanish makes sense. Ensenada, just because that's where my daddy sent me."

"You didn't have to learn Spanish in boarding school? I had to learn three languages at my boarding school."

She knew he'd attended the best boarding school in the US from around the age of twelve, Boston University for his undergrad followed by his MBA at Stanford. The man was no slouch.

"No. I learned Latin." She actually did know Latin, along with Spanish, French, sign language, and some Russian. Between the Marines and the CIA, she'd been provided with a top-notch education. Not that she could tell him that.

"Latin isn't very practical."

"Not in conversation, no. But it's been very beneficial in other areas of study. Many root words are from Latin."

"What about college? Your school didn't require a foreign language—that wasn't dead?" he quipped with a grin.

"My college roommate was deaf, so I chose sign language as my foreign language requirement." That part was true. When she was getting her undergraduate degree, she quickly grew tired of having to write everything down in order to communicate with her hearing-impaired roommate.

"So how much Spanish do you know?"

"Not much—you've seen my skills. But that's why my daddy sent me here. He said the best way to learn is to be immersed in the culture."

"That's what I've found."

There was nothing out of the ordinary with his questions, but there was just something about the way he looked at her when he asked them that had her on edge. She needed to keep her wits about her so as not to get tripped up.

She decided to steer the conversation back to him.

"What about you? What do you do? Judging by your expensive taste in watches and whiskey, not to mention your beautiful home, it must be important."

His file said he had various standard answers to that question. She was curious which he'd use today.

"I'm the chief financial officer of my family's business."

She hadn't read that one in his file.

"Oh. That sounds important," she teased. "What's your family's business?"

"Mainly drug exports."

This was definitely something new. She tilted her head. "Anything I've heard of? They come out with the oddest names for drugs these days and then advertise them with a catchy jingle. Then there's some side effects that get them sued, and you never see the commercial again."

"Hmm, mostly cocaine and marijuana. Some heroin, meth on occasion."

Wait. What did he just say?

"I'm—" She stammered. She wasn't prepared for him to just blurt that out. Why would he do something like that? She needed to react like he'd expect Ruby, a Texas oil heiress, would. She put her hand to her chest in her best 'I'm shocked' posture and gasped, "Your family business is illegal *drugs*?"

"Well, not completely, but that's the majority of it. We also dabble in arms sales, some human smuggling, murder-for-hire..."

She stood staring at him with her mouth open, unsure why he'd be telling her all this. What was he up to? Was he going to try and kill her?

He reached under her chin and pushed up to close her mouth.

"I'm teasing you, *Bella*. You should see your face right now."

"That's... that's not funny, Dante. My daddy would not approve of me being with a man who sells drugs."

She purposefully sounded naïve about the cartel's role as *supplier*—not necessarily *seller*.

Obviously, he didn't correct her but casually added as they started walking. "We are exploring investment options in medical marijuana dispensaries in the U.S."

That wasn't in the Guzman cartel file, and she wondered if it was true. He had thrown her off-balance and gotten the upper hand, so she needed to even things out. Bending over so her ass was high in the air, she 'fixed' the strap of her sandal, then stood up, knowing full well he had been staring at her butt.

Dante came up behind her, wrapped his arm around her waist, and pulled her against him, his hand slipping down to cup her mons. She felt his hard cock against her ass, and heard the amusement in his voice as he murmured in her ear,

"Do you think your daddy would approve of all the dirty things I've already done to his little girl?"

She subtly pushed her ass against his cock and wiggled. "I can say with certainty, he would not. As a matter of fact, I think there would be a shotgun involved somehow."

Ruby felt his chest rumble as he laughed out loud. He nipped her earlobe and ground his cock against her. "Then it should probably be our little secret. Because I have an adversity to guns but definitely an affinity to doing dirty things with you." As if to emphasize his point, his grip on her front tightened, and he thrust once, hard, before releasing her.

He reached for her hand, and they began walking again. In the path ahead, she could see the colorful garden with dozens of varieties of flowers that she'd noticed while having breakfast on the terraced patio. She had been right—his estate was breathtaking during the daytime.

"My God," she murmured as they approached the beautiful flowers, "how many landscapers do you have on staff?"

He slowed his pace and cocked his head. "I'm not really sure. I would guess quite a few, but I leave that to my head gardener."

"Really? That surprises me that you don't know the exact number and number of hours each person works."

"Why? I have no problem delegating once people have proven they're dependable and trustworthy. I hire good people to oversee things and then get out of their way." He gestured to their surroundings. "As you can see, it's working."

Ruby thought that was the perfect time to ask about security without rousing his suspicions but tried to be nonchalant, leaning over and smelling a large yellow rose growing on one of the many bushes.

"That can't be with all of your staff. You have to know everyone who is on your security detail."

"No, not everyone. Just the men I come in direct contact with. I trust that José, the head of my security team does his due diligence and makes sure to only hire people we can trust. He's very thorough and takes his job seriously."

Probably because his life depended on it, she mused. Fucking up a cartel's security was a sure-fire way to find yourself hanging from a bridge.

Still, she made a mental note to report back that security and landscaping were vulnerable points.

"So you really don't know how many people you have employed here, between your landscaping and security staff. What about housekeeping?"

"Rosa and Maria have been with me since I was a child. If they need extra help, I trust them to hire whomever they want. It's usually someone they're related to... their daughters, granddaughters, nieces..."

That would explain why the women doted on him.

"I assume you take pretty good care of them."

He chuckled. "You could say that. Not many housekeepers in Ensenada live in the neighborhoods they do or send their children to the private schools their children went to."

"No wonder they love you so much."

He shrugged. "The feeling is mutual. I've known them my whole life, so I have great affection for them both. Not to mention, it's in my best interest to make sure the women taking care of me and my home are well taken care of themselves. I don't know what I'm going to do when they want to retire."

You'll probably be in prison by then.

The thought made her sad, which was troublesome. Fortunately for her, her assignment was to bring about Enrique's removal from the Guzman cartel not obtain evidence for Dante's prosecution. It seemed like the CIA had come to terms with drug cartels in Mexico—they just wanted ones that weren't so ruthless.

She sat down on a stone bench overlooking a fountain with angels spouting water from various body parts.

"So, do you bring all your dates here?" she teased.

Dante sat down next to her, his face serious. "I told you last night, I don't bring women to my home. I usually *entertain* at a hotel."

Ruby frowned in disbelief. "I think I'm going to call bullshit. You just met me last night and you brought me here.

I find it hard to believe that I'm anyone special compared to the women you've dated."

She shouldn't be challenging him. She just couldn't help herself.

"I can't explain it," he said quietly as he watched the water spurt from a cherub's mouth. "There's just something special about you that calls to me." He turned to look at her with a solemn expression. "I'd like to think the feeling isn't one-sided."

She stared at him for a beat before answering softly, "No, it's not one-sided."

"Besides, you're one to talk," the corner of his mouth turned up. "Miss, my-daddy-raised-me-not-to-get-in-cars-with-strangers. Might I remind you that you not only got in the back of my limo, but spread your legs within five minutes and were eagerly choking on my Mexican swizzle stick ten minutes after that."

Her cheeks burned at his recollection of how their car ride transpired. It wasn't exactly inaccurate, just didn't paint a very flattering picture of her.

"I don't know what you're talking about," she quipped with a smirk as she stood up and walked away. "I'm a lady, Señor Guzman," she called over her shoulder.

He quickly followed, reaching out to pull her body back against his. "But you were a beautiful whore in my bed last night," he growled in her ear. "I've never met anyone who has perfected the dichotomy better."

She spun in his arms, her hands on his biceps. "The same could be said for you too, you know. Gentleman by day, aggressive, callous dom by night."

He jerked his head back. "You think I'm callous?"

"Well, I—"

He interrupted. "I'll give you aggressive and dominant, perhaps even base and vulgar at times. But callous?"

He seemed genuinely upset.

"I'm sorry. Callous was the wrong word. I should have said, aggressive, *passionate,* deliciously dirty dom by night."

That seemed to soothe his ruffled feathers, and he grinned. "Deliciously, huh?"

Ruby cupped his cheek while staring into his eyes with a devious smile. "Oh, most definitely."

Chapter Six

Ruby

It was mid-afternoon, and Dante hadn't left her side, showing her the estate—inside and out then lounging with her poolside for lunch. She didn't know if that was a good sign or not. He either was enjoying spending time with her, or he didn't trust her. Maybe it was a little of both. She could relate.

"Do you want to go swimming?"

"My swimsuit is at the hotel." She looked at him pointedly. "Along with the other things I wasn't allowed to get last night."

He ignored her attempted dig. "Who said anything about bathing suits?"

She let out a huff worthy of the debutante she was supposed to be, complete with tossing her hair over her shoulder. "I am not skinny dipping in the middle of the day."

He cocked his head with a grin. "But you will at night? Good to know."

"I didn't say that."

"You implied it."

She rolled her eyes but couldn't help but laugh. The idea had its merits.

Dante reached for her hand across the table, returning her smile. "How about I have my driver take you to your hotel, so you can pack your things, including your swimsuit. Enough for maybe a few days, at least."

He'd said it as a statement, but his raised eyebrows and sheepish grin let her know it really was a question. Things were going better than she could have planned. Still, she knew not to appear too eager.

"A few days? You sure you won't be sick of me by tomorrow?"

He let go of her hand and rubbed his chin as he mock-contemplated her question. "I suppose it's a possibility. You are a little bossy." The corner of his mouth hitched in a wicked grin. "But your cock sucking skills and delicious pussy make it tolerable."

"So you're saying you just want me around so you can fuck me?" she teased.

He brought his bottom lip up toward his nose and nodded. "Yeah. Pretty much."

She rolled her eyes with pursed lips. "Gee, how could I turn down such a romantic offer?"

"You can't."

Dante stood, came around to her side of the table, and reached for her hand again. When she was standing, he wrapped one arm around her and held her hand, swaying their bodies to a melody only he could hear.

"In all serious, Ruby Rhodes, I've been having such a wonderful time getting to know you, I'm not ready for our time together to end."

"Just because I go back to my hotel doesn't mean it has to end."

"Perhaps. But I'm a selfish man and am enjoying having you all to myself."

"Don't you have to work?"

He shrugged. "Here and there. I can breakaway while you're enjoying the pool. I do most of my business from my office in the house."

Good to know.

"So?" he asked, looking down at her. "Would you like to be my guest for a few days? You could even check out of your hotel and bring everything here—that way you're not incurring any expenses for a room you're not using."

"I don't think you realize how much stuff I have," she said with a laugh.

"I have a whole suite you can store your things in. Of course, you'll still sleep in my bed."

She smirked. "Of course."

She had been surprised that he'd spent the entire night with her last night, allowing her to stay until morning in his bed. Intel had suggested that wasn't normally the case. His companions didn't stay until the next day. Whether that was his doing or theirs had never been determined, but naturally, she had assumed his and had been prepared to be asked to leave last night. When he took her to his house, she was still expecting that after sex, he would have her sleep in another room not in his arms.

Ruby had to admit—it'd been a pleasant surprise to wake up this morning next to his hard body, and the idea of doing that for the next few days was not without merit.

"Okay, I'll go get my things."

****

Dante

"What the hell happened to fucking her and kicking her to the curb?" John asked incredulously when Dante told him she was coming to stay for a few days. Longer, if Dante had anything to say about it, but, first things first. "Jesus Christ, I leave the hemisphere for a few weeks and look what happens to you."

Dante could almost see his friend on the other end, shaking his head.

"I've decided to go with a different tactic. At least until we find out why she's here and who she really is."

"I'm guessing you've either had sex and she blew your mind, or you haven't had sex but are planning on putting the moves on her."

"Option A."

"Yeah," John chuckled. "I figured as much. Still, not only are you sleeping with the enemy, you're moving her into your home?"

"I have my reasons."

"Care to enlighten me?"

Dante debated how much of his plan he wanted to tell John, in case he failed miserably.

"I'm going to make her fall in love with me," he confided quietly.

"You know she's literally trained not to do that, right? Like, you might think you're playing her, but you'll be the one who is getting played."

"How is that possible when I already know what she's up to? Any word on why she's here or who she really is?"

"The inside guy is working on it, but he's already let me know it isn't going to be cheap since not only could he lose his job, but he'd be looking at prison if he were caught."

"We expected that."

"I'm just reminding you, so when you notice my spending is sky-high this month, you'll remember that's why."

"When have I ever questioned you or even given a shit about your spending?"

"Well, there's a first time for everything. And South America hasn't exactly been cheap either, so you need to take that into consideration when you look at my expenses. Don't freak out."

"When it comes to you? I'm not worried."

John was his oldest, most trusted friend. The two men were like brothers, and he was the one person Dante could count on to make sure shit was handled right... the first time. In turn, Dante never batted an eye at his friend's spending.

"How do you know he's not skimming from us?" Enrique once questioned during one of the many meetings where he shot down everything Dante suggested about legitimizing the business more.

Dante had just shrugged. "I guess I don't. If he is, it's so negligible that I don't even give a shit if he is. Which he's not because he has no reason to."

Both Dante and John were almost forty and already had more money than they'd ever spend in their lifetimes. Hell, their children's lifetimes—if either ever had kids.

Still, his uncle—who was fiercely fighting any effort to legitimize the cartel—was skeptical. "Keep an eye on him."

Yeah, okay.

Dante didn't even dignify it with his usual line of nodding his head and agreeing to placate the older man. It was apparent his uncle was becoming a liability to the organization, something Enrique's younger brother, Ramon eluded to when he stopped by Dante's not long after his meeting with Enrique.

No one wanted to come right out and say Enrique needed to go, in case the other was loyal to *El Jefe*. But Dante recognized Ramon's fishing expedition for what it was— feeling him out about a possible takeover. Dante cautiously took the bait and the wheels of ousting Enrique and putting Ramon in power were put in motion.

Both Ramon and Dante knew what that would mean—Enrique's execution because the older Guzman would not give up his power any other way.

So when John called later that night with the details of why 'Ruby' was sent to him, Dante decided he was definitely keeping her around. Using her until she carried out her mission was just an added benefit.

Chapter Seven

Ruby

Her time at Dante's estate so far had been almost like a honeymoon, of sorts. They had breakfast together every morning on the patio, talking politics, pop culture, and everything else under the sun. Dante was very well-read and had a lot of interesting opinions, and she found herself intrigued by his observations and take on things in the world. Then he'd excuse himself to work for a few hours, and she'd lounge by the pool on her computer, posting on her fake social media and covertly sending messages to her handler, or she worked out in his personal gym. She needed to keep in shape, and while sex with Dante burned a lot of calories, it wasn't exactly going to keep her ready for a fight. Ruby also spent a little time in the kitchen, under the guise of practicing her Spanish, hoping to hear some dirt on him from the staff. A fruitless endeavor—they adored their employer. When he returned in the afternoons, they would either relax by the pool or take a stroll around the grounds. He'd taken her into Ensenada once for lunch and shopping. And they fucked morning, noon, and night.

If he weren't her mark, she could see herself falling for him.

Except he *was* her mark—a means to Enrique. Not to mention a criminal, and she was a government agent sworn to uphold the law. But he was such a gentleman, well, except for when they were naked. But that just made it that much hotter because she knew he would revert back to being respectful and treating her deferentially when she wanted him to. Besides, he'd never want her if he knew who she really was, so falling for him for real was out of the question.

"You love being my whore, admit it," he'd growled one afternoon while fingering her pussy in the pool house. Her ass was high in the air as she sucked his cock on her hands and knees on the changing bench next to him.

She slurped off his cock and panted, "I love being your whore," then resumed her oral attention to his dick.

He chuckled, almost sinisterly. "Oh, if your friends only knew what a slut you really are..."

Kennedy didn't have friends, so frankly, she didn't give a shit. But Ruby was supposed to have a lot of friends 'in society' so she needed to respond appropriately. Besides, their game only turned her on more anyway.

"Thank you for keeping my secret, sir."

"Good whores get rewarded, Ruby. And bad sluts... what do they get?"

She pulled his cock out of her mouth to answer dutifully. "Punished."

With his other hand, he yanked the back of her hair hard, so her head was tilted back, sending a ripple of pleasure and pain down her spine at once as she stared up at him. "Punished, what?"

"Punished, *sir.*"

Dante murmured, "Good girl," then directed her head back to his cock and added a third finger into her pussy, stretching her full. "I think I would enjoy punishing you, though, Bella."

When his thumb probed her backdoor, triggering her orgasm, she conceded, she probably would enjoy being punished by him, too.

****

Dante

He'd lost track of how many times he'd come in the last four days. But he fucked her every chance he got: in the garden, against a tree, in the pool house, in the Jacuzzi, in the car, in his bed, even in his office yesterday after hanging up the phone with John who'd called to tell him why she was really there. Dante had summoned her and fucked her face without mercy. She took it like a champ, and when he dipped his fingers under her dress, he found her soaked. She was such a natural submissive—at least to him. But he doubted there were many men who could tame her like he had.

Actually, the thought of any man fucking touching her made his blood boil.

I need to be careful, he chastised himself on more than one occasion. *She's not fucking real, and she doesn't really belong with me.*

But she made it so easy for Dante to forget that she didn't really belong with him. He wondered if she sometimes forgot too. He called her *Ruby* when he fucked her to help serve as a reminder—which usually made him punish her. But then she'd enjoy it, and so would he.

"Rosa said it's your birthday on Friday," she said at dinner Monday evening.

"She did?"

"Yes. And that it's a big birthday, but you aren't having a party?"

Dante hadn't wanted a party. Period. But he especially didn't want one without his best friend there. However, Ruby didn't know anything about John—that Dante was aware of—and he preferred to keep it that way. For now, at least.

And he'd just learned her real name—Kennedy Alicia Jones, complete with pictures of the rundown trailer she supposedly grew up in in Fargo, North Dakota. It was a far cry from the mansion in Houston she'd described. His private investigator was gathering more information, but he could only imagine how hard she must have worked to get out of there and start a better life for herself.

"I'd much rather celebrate by whisking you off somewhere exotic and fucking you senseless."

"What did you have in mind?" she asked with a coy smile.

"It's a surprise."

And that's how he ended up on a beach in Belize, balls deep in her just before midnight on the eve of his fortieth birthday. The warm ocean lapping around their bodies as they came in unison as the clock turned over into a new day.

"Happy official birthday," she whispered, her fingers in his hair as he wrapped her body tight against his, with his face buried in her neck—his cock still inside her. "You're going to have the perfect birthday weekend, I promise."

He never wanted to move from this spot—she felt like perfection underneath him.

"This is a pretty damn good start to my fortieth year."

He picked his head up and looked down at her beautiful face—her cheeks were flush from her orgasm, but her expression was tender when she gazed back at him as he stroked her jawline with his fingertip.

"Who knew I'd be in love for the first time on my fortieth birthday," he quipped softly while studying her carefully for her reaction.

And for the first time since he ran into her outside the bar and she uttered, *"Discúlpame,"* did Ruby Rhodes screw up.

"Who knew I'd be in love for the first time at thirty-six."

He cocked his head and narrowed his eyes, even though he already knew that. "You're thirty-six? I thought you said you were twenty-eight."

She could certainly pass for it, but he'd doubted from the beginning that a twenty-eight year old would rank high enough in the CIA to be given the assignment she was in. When he was given the initial information on her and learned her real age, it made more sense. He liked her being closer to his age.

To his shock, she didn't try to lie her way out of her admission.

"Um, yes?" She bit her bottom lip as she poised her answer as a question with a grimace. "I'm sorry I lied."

Dante decided to push her, just to see how much she'd confess. He was hoping for everything, if she really did love him. She'd already fucked up royally, admitting her age. Ruby's background check said she was twenty-eight, how was she going to explain that?

To his disappointment, she went back into character. "I didn't want you to think poorly of me. I haven't exactly accomplished much with my life, other than live off my father's money."

She chose to continue the lie, and that pissed him off although he tried to mask it with a closed mouth smile. He'd played this all wrong. His plan had backfired because he was in love with her—at least the woman she'd let him fall in love with.

The one that's fake. Still, he couldn't help but think about the determined little girl from Fargo who'd gotten herself out of poverty. He'd loved her even more, knowing that about her.

Yet she'd revealed a part of herself tonight—something real—and that meant something, as far as he was concerned.

"I don't think poorly of you. But I am disappointed you lied to me." *And continue to lie to me.* He gripped her hair tight and murmured in her ear, "What do bad sluts get, *Ruby*?" He emphasized her fake-name purely for his satisfaction—saying it out loud somehow made him feel like he wasn't getting played.

"Punished," she whispered.

He pinched her nipple, hard. "Punished, *what*?"

"Punished, *sir*."

"Good girl."

He then released her hair and nipple abruptly, massaging where he'd just been tugging, and with a smirk, lowered his mouth inches from hers.

"Now let's talk about that other thing…"

Chapter Eight

Ruby

She'd been scolding herself all week for being so dreamy-eyed around him. She needed to keep her head in the game and focus on the mission. She'd already been censured for not planting any surveillance equipment in his house.

"I'm not risking it," she'd told the agency when they gave her grief about it. "He's already said he sweeps his place regularly for that type of equipment. If something were to show up now, his suspicions would be focused squarely on me. He's just starting to trust me; I don't want to jeopardize that."

Kennedy really didn't want to risk what was building between them, but the truth was, she didn't want the CIA to be able to gather evidence against Dante either. Especially not from the sanctity of his home. She had come to cherish the estate as well—invading that just felt... wrong.

"Agent Jones, you need to be sure you're separating yourself from your Ruby Rhodes persona," her handler warned.

"That's not a problem. I'm a professional," she said dismissively. "I am, however, going to be making a large purchase on my persona's credit card. Dante's birthday is coming up, and I need to get him an expensive present."

"You've been given carte blanche with your expenses on this assignment, you know that."

"Just want to make sure there's no misunderstanding."

She couldn't afford to pay for the TAG Heuer she was planning on buying him. Well, she *could* afford it, technically, she'd just rather not be on the hook for the purchase.

She'd bought it the next day and had it engraved with, *Happy 40th*. She couldn't bring herself to have the name *Ruby* engraved on it, so she left it at that. She was originally going to say something about Macallan Cask but decided to just buy him a bottle instead, and almost gave it to him a day early, on his private jet, when their flight attendant came back after taking their drink order, shaking her head.

"I think you finished the bottle last time and flight services replenished it with regular Macallan."

Dante chuckled. "I'll have to make sure they only charged me for regular then." With a nod of his head, he added, "Macallan is fine for me. Ruby, do you want something else?"

"No, I'll have the same."

His jet was beautiful, and she tried acting like it wasn't her first time on a private aircraft. She'd flown commercial for what felt like hundreds of times—even first class if the assignment required it, and of course, during her time in the Marines she'd done her fair share of jumping out of planes, but she'd never been up in the air in something so luxurious. However, an oil heiress would have, so she couldn't gawk.

Still, he asked, "Is this your first time on a private jet?"

"Oh, no," she said dismissively. "My daddy's company has two. But they're supposed to be for company business, so Daddy doesn't use them much for personal use."

"Yes, I'm sure there's a lot of tax laws one has to follow the U.S." He didn't sound convinced.

Changing the subject, she asked sweetly, "So, you said to bring my passport, where are we off to, Birthday Boy?"

"Birthday *Man,* sweetheart. I'm all man," he corrected with a grin to let her know his offense was in jest.

"Mmm, yes you are," she purred in his ear and squeezed his inner thigh while rubbing her tits against his arm.

"Careful, princess. We've got a four-hour flight—I will have no problem taking you to the bedroom and fucking you the entire time."

"I know you'd have no *problem.* You've proven you're quite capable of that. But you still haven't answered the question—where are we going?"

"Belize. I've rented a bungalow that walks out to the beach. There's snorkeling on the reef, rainforest excursions, or just lounging around on the beach or by the pool. Whatever you want to do."

"Baby, it's *your* birthday. We'll do whatever you want."

"What I want is to see you happy and having a good time."

His kindness only made her feel more conflicted. Her guilty feelings for betraying him had her stomach in knots. She was falling in love with a criminal—the man whose uncle she was sent to assassinate. She either didn't go through with her mission, effectively ending her career, or she completed it and ruined any chance she might have with Dante.

Not that she really believed she had a chance. Even if she didn't go through with killing Enrique, she highly doubted Dante would want to be with her if he found out the truth, and the CIA would most definitely have her working behind a desk somewhere like Podunk, Alaska. There was only play here—complete her mission. With renewed determination, she dozed off next to him thirty-five thousand feet in the air.

It was late when they got to their bungalow, but it was a beautiful night, so they took a walk by the ocean to decompress, and the next thing she knew—they were having sex on the beach.

Then Dante had to go and tell her he's in love with her, and she found herself blurting out the same, divulging some truth about herself in the process.

Revealing her true age had just slipped out, momentarily overwhelmed with his admission, and how happy it made her. It scared her how easy it was to sometimes forget that he was the cartel's moneyman, and she worked for the CIA, and this was all a big lie.

"When did you realize you were in love with me?" he asked with a cocky grin.

She was so fucked. And not the good kind like she had been for the past ten days. It was the between-a-rock-and-a-hard-place kind.

"Ruby?" his voice brought her back to reality, and his question he was still waiting on an answer to.

"I think I've slowly fallen for you from the start, but I knew for sure Wednesday night."

The corner of his mouth lifted in a smile at the memory. "Ah, Wednesday night. I was hoping you'd say that. That's when I was certain, too. I almost told you, but it felt like you already knew."

"I did."

Wednesday night he'd made love to her. Not his usual dominant, aggressive style that she was starting to crave, but slow, stare in her eyes and kiss her passionately while he tenderly took his time and savored her kind of lovemaking. Afterwards, he'd held her like he always did, kissing her hair and murmuring words of adoration, but things between them had been forever changed—and she knew they had both felt it.

She'd almost confessed everything right then, but each time she'd started to form the words, she stopped. He would never forgive her for betraying him and all coming clean would do is compromise the mission. And now, here she was, with an ass crack full of sand and not a clue how she was going to fix the mess she'd just made.

There really was no fixing it. This was going to end with a terrible betrayal—there was no other way. All she could do was enjoy the ride while it lasted and be grateful for the memories of her time with him.

He rolled off her and stood, pulling his shorts up then brushing the sand from his elbows and knees before extending his hand to help her up. "Come on, baby. Let's go back to the bungalow."

"Yeah, we probably should get some sleep. We have a big day of celebrating tomorrow."

"Who said anything about sleeping?" he asked with a wink.

Ruby smirked. "Whatever you want, Birthday Boy."

"Man," he corrected.

She stood on her tiptoes and whispered huskily in his ear, "Your wish is my desire, Birthday *Man*." Wiggling her butt uncomfortably, she added with a cheeky grin, "But I really need to shower first. I have sand in places no one ever should."

****

Dante

They stayed up until the early morning hours fucking, talking, and making love. He could feel her internal conflict as she lay in his arms, her head on his chest while he told her about his childhood and in turn, asked her about hers and especially when he projected about their future.

She played along, but her tone was wistful when she whispered, "That sounds perfect." He noticed his chest felt damp *before* she ran her tongue along his pecs with a seductive smile, then trailed down his stomach to his cock where she distracted him with another epic blowjob.

"Fuuuck, woman," he panted when she pointed his cock at her tits herself and finished him off, smearing his seed into her skin like a fucking porn star would.

He decided to dangle Enrique in front of her right before they fell asleep. He'd learned of her mission earlier this week—the day before he learned her true identity. Fortunately, her mission actually worked into his and Ramon's plans, and he would probably tell her as much when she finally confessed to him. *If* she finally confessed to him.

"Maybe I should have a belated birthday party, so I can introduce you to my family. I'm sure my father and uncles will be instantly smitten—just like I was, and the women will love you even more than Rosa or Maria, if that's possible."

Instead of snatching at the bait and running with it, she hesitated. "I think we should wait before I meet your family."

Yeah, she really loves me, he thought smugly. She was going to be spilling her guts before the weekend was over.

"Why do you want to wait?"

"I don't know. I guess things are going so well between us, I don't want to jinx it." She lifted her head with a smirk. "Because then you'll want to meet *my* family, and they're a train wreck. And my daddy will hate you, and then I'll have to choose between you or him." She rambled on theatrically, "And it'll just be a disaster because I'll choose you, and then I'll be cut out of the will..." She laid her head back down on

his chest and snuggled closer. "Let's just stay in our little bubble for a little while longer."

He could read between the lines—her 'daddy' was really the CIA, and she was going to have to choose between her agency and him.

"Don't worry about being cut out of the will, baby," he murmured with his lips to her hair. "I've got more than enough money to take care of you."

Dante meant that. He'd love to take care of her, if she chose him.

"It's not really about the money, Dante. I have plenty in savings."

"Hey wait..." he cut her off. "Why would your father hate me? Is he racist?"

Ruby lifted her head again. "What? No. He sent me to Mexico, didn't he?"

"Why then?"

Her smirk was back. "Because you sell drugs, remember?" Throwing his 'joke' from when they first met back at him.

"Oh, yeah. That." He sighed dramatically like he was going along with her act. Yet, it felt like, somehow, they were communicating the truth through this game. "Would it make a difference if my company were more reputable, and we owned other businesses besides our illegal ones?"

She traced her finger along his shoulder. "No. Just the fact that you sold drugs will make him not like you."

"Darn it."

"Yeah," she agreed, melancholy in her voice.

"I guess we'll have to figure something else out." Dante squeezed her shoulders. "Okay, baby. We'll stay in the bubble until we do."

She sounded sleepy when she murmured, "Maybe we can just live here forever."

If he thought that was all it would take, he'd make it happen. But he knew better. It wasn't going to be that easy.

Chapter Nine

Dante

He was roused from his slumber with his cock hard as steel. It took a minute for him to register why, until he realized it was her warm mouth sliding up and down his shaft.

Touching her hair softly, he opened his eyes.

"I could wake up to that sight for the next forty years," he quipped with a sleepy smile.

"Good morning," she murmured, pulling his shaft from her mouth to stroke him up and down while she looked at him from between his legs with a smile. "Happy birthday."

He put his hands behind his head to watch her. "It's starting out pretty damn good—ever since the clock struck midnight. Best birthday yet."

She swirled her tongue along his helmet. "Oh, baby. We're just getting started." She paused and lifted her head. "Unless you're too old to keep up now?"

He was on her in an instant, flipping her onto her stomach on top of a pillow then pinning her body in place with the weight of his. Grinding his cock against the crack of her ass, he growled in her ear, "What do bad sluts get, Ruby?"

He felt her lift her hips and press back against him. "Mmm, punished," she purred.

"It's not punishment if you like it, baby," he said with a chuckle.

"What if I love it?"

He closed his eyes and let out a low groan. "You are so fucking perfect."

She lifted her hips again—well, as much as she could with his body on hers.

"What do you want, princess?" he teased, pushing his cock against her ass.

"To get fucked." She waited a beat then added, "Sir."

"Where should I fuck you?"

"Oh, god. I don't care. Just fuck me, please."

There wasn't any coconut oil handy, otherwise, he'd take that as an invitation and be inside her ass in a heartbeat. Coconut oil was definitely going on the shopping list for later today.

Dante rolled on a condom he'd grabbed from the nightstand and slid inside her soaked pussy as they both moaned in unison. Her closed legs heightened the sensation, and in a plank position, he slammed into her hard and deep.

"Oh my god, baby! That feels so good," she moaned.

Thankfully, he worked his core a lot, so he was able to maintain his plank while he thrust into her rapidly. She lifted her ass slightly, and he dropped to his knees and slapped her pale skin until her butt was a nice shade of pink, before sliding inside her again.

"Yessss," she cooed.

Her pussy was extra tight in this position, and he dropped to one knee for leverage. He wasn't going to last much longer, and judging by how wet she was, she wasn't either.

"Don't stop," she begged. "Oh, god, please don't stop."

He gave her ass another hard slap. "Please don't stop, *what*?"

"Please don't stop, sir."

"Are you going to come, little slut?"

"Yes," she whimpered.

"Good. Come for me. Come all over my cock, baby."

He felt her body tense up, then completely relax as she let out a long moan.

Thrusting hard and fast, his orgasm was right behind hers, and he held her hips tight while he came balls deep inside her.

Dante dropped his forehead on her back as he caught his breath.

"You really have no idea what you do to this old man."

He felt her giggle when he went to pull out. Except she squeezed her thighs together, so he couldn't.

"No! Don't go!"

"Baby, I'd like nothing more than to stay inside your sweet pussy all day." He dropped onto his forearms and enveloped her body with his. "But I need to take care of the condom."

She relaxed her thighs, grumbling, "Fine. But hurry back."

He returned and spooned her tiny body tight against his. They lay like that for a few blissful minutes, and Ruby let out a contented sigh. "I really do love you."

Dante believed her—and he also believed it was causing her a great deal of stress.

He kissed her shoulder. "I know. I love you, too, princess."

"As much as I want to just lie here all day with your arms around me, we probably should get up. We have a big day of celebrating ahead."

He rolled off her and propped his elbow on the bed to rest his head on his knuckles while he watched her slowly roll over. "Should we start with breakfast?"

She quickly glanced over at him. "Do you even have to ask?"

Dante laughed out loud as he leaned down to kiss her temple. "That's my girl."

****

Ruby

I'm his girl. This was so bad. And yet, so, so good.

She'd decided she was going to enjoy his birthday weekend, revel in being in love, and not worry about a damn thing except making sure he wore a condom when he fucked her. The last thing she needed was a baby Guzman in her belly. A birth control implant or even pills would have worked so much better than relying on condoms in her line of work, but she'd tried them all, and they had really fucked with her hormones—to the point that she would cry at the drop of a hat, so that quickly ended that.

Emotions had no place in her profession. At least, they weren't supposed to.

I am so fucked.

She chided herself—*Not gonna worry about that until we get back to Ensenada.*

This weekend, she was going to be Ruby Rhodes and enjoy her time with the only man she'd ever fallen in love with. She wasn't going to allow herself to think about their expiration date.

They stayed on the patio of their bungalow after they finished breakfast, and she smiled brightly at him. "I got you a present."

He cocked his head. "You did? Why? I have everything I need."

Reaching into her purse, she pulled out the professionally wrapped gift and handed it to him. "Because I love you, and I wanted to."

She was going to get in as many *I love yous* she could while they were still in the bubble.

Dante stared at the package in his hands for a long minute, then slowly lifted his head to look at her. When he did, he was beaming.

"Wow. Thank you. This is really thoughtful."

"You don't even know what it is!"

"Still, you took the time to get me a present..."

She cocked her head and furrowed her brows. "It's your birthday. Of course I got you a present." What kind of asshole did he think she was?

"I just don't get a lot of birthday presents."

"Well, that's obviously going to change now that I'm in your life."

Ruby clapped her hands when he lifted the box to his ear and shook it. He smirked and set it on the table when she started to bounce up and down in her seat.

"Oh my god! Open it!"

With a wink he ripped off the wrapping paper and opened the lid of the box then stared at the watch for a long time before lifting his eyes to hers, not saying a word.

Her face fell. "You hate it. I knew I should have bought you another Rolex."

Dante immediately reached for her hand across the table. "No! I don't want another Rolex—this is perfect. I just can't believe you bought me this. I fucking love it."

She tried to act humble and shrugged. "I just know how much you like nice watches and thought this would be a perfect addition to your collection."

Dante pulled it from the grey velvet inlay to examine it closer.

"I had it engraved," she said quietly, wanting to kick herself for not having something more sentimental inscribed.

He turned it over, and his brows knitted together as he read the inscription. "You didn't include your name."

"I know, I'm sorry. I didn't realize I'd forgotten that part until I got it home." It was a lie, but it wasn't like she could tell him why she hadn't wanted to include her name.

There was something about the way he nodded at her explanation then glanced at her out of the corner of his eye that struck her as odd. He quickly covered it up with a smile and leaned over to kiss her cheek. "That's okay. It's not like I can forget who gave it to me."

"I hope not."

"Not a chance."

He took his Rolex off and slid it into the box, then fastened the TAG Heuer around his wrist. Holding his arm away from his body, he twisted his wrist as if to catch the light from different angles to admire his new timepiece.

"This is my new favorite."

"Really?"

He leaned over and kissed her softly on the lips. "By far, baby. I love it."

It was ridiculous how happy that made her.

Dante stood, the box in one hand while he reached for her hand to help her up with the other. Instead of taking his offered hand, she held hers out. "I can put that in my bag."

"Oh, thanks."

Ruby dropped the box in her oversized purse and stood up while he made a show of trying to peer inside her bag.

"What all do you have in there, Mary Poppins? I mean, besides the kitchen sink."

"Ha ha. You won't be laughing if you need a Band-Aid or a granola bar later though."

"You need that big of a purse for a Band-Aid and a granola bar?" he teased.

"There's other stuff too," she said, turning her body away from him as she zipped it up.

"Like what?"

They both reached for each other's hand at the same time, then started walking toward the beach without discussing their destination, as if they both felt the pull of the water.

"I don't know. Just stuff. Didn't your mom ever carry a purse?"

"Yes, and I wasn't allowed in it. So women's purses are like an exotic mystery for me now."

She chuckled at his fascination. "I'll let you in on a little secret. There's nothing that interesting in my bag."

"Aw, don't spoil the illusion."

"What do you *think* is in here?"

"In *your* purse? I don't know. Dildos? Lingerie? An umbrella? Listening devices?"

She tried not to react specifically to 'listening devices'. It would seem suspicious—although it was odd that he would bring something like that up, even in a joking manner.

"Why, on God's green earth, would I have any of those things—other than maybe the umbrella?"

He shrugged with a grin. "I would think a dildo would be far more useful than an umbrella."

Ruby let go of his hand and wrapped her arms around his biceps with a smug grin. "What do I need a dildo for? You tapping out on me already, old man?"

The birthday man pfffted. "Not a chance, princess. Not a chance."

Chapter Ten

Dante

"Why on earth would I have any of those things?" Ruby asked like she was astonished at such an idea.

I don't know, maybe because you're a fucking spy?

He didn't say that, of course. He'd continue to play her game while still occasionally lobbing some big, fat beach balls in her court with the hopes she'd eventually spike one and come clean.

No luck so far.

Regardless, the day had been perfect. He couldn't have scripted a better birthday.

Fucking the woman he's in love with at midnight when the day became official—check.

Being woken up with her mouth on his cock—check.

Receiving an amazing, thoughtful birthday present from her—check.

Snorkeling with her on the reef and enjoying watching her marvel at all the sea life while she's in her bikini—check.

Slipping away and fucking her behind a dune—check.

Eating a delicious birthday meal at a 5-Star restaurant—check.

Fingering the most beautiful woman in the room's pussy under the table—check.

Eating said pussy for dessert in their private bungalow on the beach—check.

Having his cock sucked in a side alley on their way back to the bungalow from the restaurant—check.

Ending the day with her bare-breasted, in his arms, the scent of her filling his senses while she whispered she loved him—check.

Like he said, perfect day.

If only she were real—or at least confide in him she was really Kennedy Jones.

He kissed her hair and sighed. For this weekend only, he decided it didn't matter.

Ruby lifted her head to look at him. "That was a big sigh."

"Just sad the day has to come to an end."

She began laying soft kisses on his chest. "It was a great day."

"Almost perfect."

"*Almost*? What would have made it perfect?"

He decided to lob one of those beach balls at her. "Knowing your father would approve of me dating you."

"You sell drugs, remember?"

Technically, I supply them to the people who sell them, sweetheart, but hey... Obviously she wasn't going to take the opening he just gave her.

"In all seriousness... do you really think your family would not approve of me?"

He decided to use the term *family* because he knew she didn't have a father growing up.

"I think..." she straddled him and kissed his neck. "I think they would meet you and fall in love with you just like I did."

He was naked under the covers, and the feel of her bare pussy on him was bringing his cock to life.

"Perfect! When do you want to introduce me?"

She dragged her lips up his neck to his ear. "Can't we just enjoy our bubble this weekend and talk about this when we get back to Ensenada? We still have two more days to try and achieve perfection."

"Baby. There isn't a thing I would have changed about today. I mean that."

"I don't think I've ever had a better day," she agreed, while brushing her stiff nipples against his chest and moving her hips in circles over his.

"I think I've created a monster," he quipped as he pulled her hips down while thrusting up between her pussy lips.

She dished it right back. "There's just something about an older man..." she purred with her lips against his. Dante reached behind her head and pulled her mouth to his—his tongue quickly exploring and tangling with hers while she continued grinding on his cock.

He pushed his cock inside her wet pussy. "We know how to fuck, huh?"

"God, yes, you do," she moaned as she began rolling her hips on his dick.

He watched her, mesmerized. Her tits bounced up and down, and she piled her hair on top of her head with her eyes closed and head thrown back while she made little whimpers and moans. It was sexy as fuck to watch her ride him.

He reached between her folds and began polishing her hard clit. That threw her rhythm off, but she leaned back on his thighs, opening her pussy a little, then quickly resumed her tempo.

If he'd learned anything about her these past ten days, it was she liked when he was dominant and aggressive, and she liked it when he talked filthy to her.

Dante slapped her inner thigh. "Spread your fucking legs."

Like the good submissive she was, she immediately slowed her pace and spread herself wider so her little pearl was peeking out at him.

He resumed rubbing her clit and chuckled when he felt her getting wetter, "Such a dirty, little slut, riding my cock with your legs spread."

She began bucking up and down on his dick while pressing her clit against his hand. Her eyes were closed tight, and she started to moan loader.

"Do you like being my dirty slut, *Ruby*?"

Channeling her inner porn star, she grabbed one tit and squeezed. "I love it, sir."

Dante gave her clit six quick slaps. "What do you love?"

"I love being your dirty whore, sir. Being used for your pleasure."

Holy fuck that's hot.

He rubbed her clit harder and faster. "Are you going to come, whore?"

She whimpered and bucked her hips faster. Dante thrust up into her.

"You better fucking come. Come right fucking now!"

He felt her pussy gush, and she chanted, "Oh my god, yes. Yes! Yes!" as her movements became uncoordinated and eventually, she collapsed forward on his chest.

Wasting no time, he quickly flipped her onto her back and began to fuck her missionary style—leaning down to suck on her stiff nipples as he did. She arched her back in reaction to his mouth on her tits and dug her fingers into his hair.

"I love how responsive you are to me," he murmured before pulling a pink bud between his teeth.

"I love everything you do to me," she moaned in response.

"That's my girl."

He cupped one tit in his hand and kneaded while he moved his mouth to her neck, never wavering in his tempo of fucking her pussy. She shocked the hell out of him by turning the tables and talking dirty to him.

"Your cock feels so good inside my pussy. Mmm... yes, sir. Please fuck me. Fuck your little slut. Give it to me."

That did the trick, and he grunted, "Where do you want it?"

"Ohhh, my tits. Please. Come on my tits."

Her words made his balls draw up, and he barely pulled out in time to paint her tits with his cum. It was more than he was expecting, considering it was the fifth time he'd come in less than twenty-four hours, and he loved the sight of her covered in his seed.

"I'm coming on your face tomorrow," he warned as he cleaned her off with a towel. "Then later on, I'm drizzling coconut oil all over you and fucking your ass while I fuck your pussy with a dildo."

She took the towel from him and wiped a spot on her side he'd missed, then tossed it toward the bathroom and snuggled in next to him.

"Mmm, baby. It's a good thing you've worn me out, otherwise I'd be up all night in anticipation."

"So fucking perfect," Dante murmured as he switched off the light and wrapped an arm around her.

He needed her to come clean with him—soon—because he wasn't fucking letting her go.

****

Ruby

She'd had more sex—with a partner—in the last ten days then she'd had in the ten years prior to meeting him. Okay, maybe not *ten* years but close to it. And still, she couldn't get enough of him. Just looking at his sexy, regal face made her want to strip off her panties and mount him or drop to her knees and worship his cock; her mood varied. And he seemed to be attuned to her needs because it felt like he adjusted from gentle love making to rough manhandling to suit what she needed. Sometimes she wouldn't even realize that had been exactly what she required until he was holding her afterwards—always completely satiated.

Unfortunately, that also meant they sometimes forgot a condom. They'd been careless more than once, but he always pulled out when he fucked her raw. Yeah, it was reckless, and she knew she was playing with fire, but in the heat of the moment, it could be hard to care. It seemed like it fit with her weekend's mantra—she'd worry about it when she got back to Ensenada.

They held hands as they walked along the beach after breakfast.

"What do you want to do today?" he asked as a seagull landed in front of them on the wet sand.

"Baby, it's your birthday weekend. What do *you* want to do today?"

"I want to take you into town, buy some coconut oil and a dildo, so I can fuck your ass and pussy at the same time like I said I was going to. Then I want to take a nap in the hammock under the palm trees outside our cabin, with your naked body on mine. When we wake up, we'll have a late lunch—maybe with a few drinks—then I'll make love to you with the windows open while the afternoon monsoon hits. When we're finished, we'll lie in bed, and you'll tell me all your secrets, and I'll tell you mine, then we'll get up and have dinner and maybe drink some more while we do a little dancing at the hotel bar. Afterwards, we'll come back here, and you'll suck my cock while you sit on my face, and we'll fall asleep with each other's cum on our faces."

She stopped walking and stared up at him with her mouth agape, unable to function at the thought of the day he just described.

Finally, she was able to form a coherent sentence. "I can't tell you how much that just turned me on. I think you've discovered the perfect day."

Well, except the telling him all her secrets part.

Dante pulled her against him. "*Bella*, yesterday was perfect. The best birthday I've ever had—by far."

"Well, then maybe we can just agree that this is going to be a perfect weekend."

The corner of his mouth turned up, and he kissed the tip of her nose. "You'll get no argument from me, my naughty slut."

Why did that turn her on so much when he called her that—and worse? She wasn't sure, maybe is assuaged her guilt? All she knew for certain was she loved it.

Ruby tugged on his hand. "Come on, we've got shopping to do."

He followed behind, murmuring, "Have I told you today how much I fucking love you?"

She was so wrecked for any other man in her future.

Chapter Eleven

Ruby

She was surprised how quickly they fell back into their routine once they returned to Ensenada. It was funny—she'd basically moved into the estate from the day after they met although neither of them had declared it out loud. After the third day she'd been there, she'd said she was going back to the hotel, and he'd simply said, "No, you're not," and that was that.

It hadn't been like she wanted to argue anyway. Staying there was perfect for the mission.

When he arrived at dinner their second night back from Belize, his jaw was set, and a scowl marred his sexy face.

"What's wrong?" she asked as he sat down at the enormous dining room table that they only occupied a fraction of.

He tossed a CIA issued bug on the table. "One of seven in my office they just found. I'm having the rest of the house and grounds swept as we speak."

Ruby swallowed hard. She hadn't planted any surveillance and wasn't sure if this was a message from her agency to her that she needed to do her job, knowing it would be found—since she'd already told them he swept for bugs regularly. Or if they were genuinely listening and checking on her to see exactly what she was up to. Either way, they'd compromised her cover, and she wasn't going to sit back and let that slide without raising a stink. But right now, she needed to figure out if Dante suspected her.

"How would it even be possible for someone to get inside here?"

"I'm not sure." He cocked his head. "Do you have any idea?"

The way he was looking at her put her on edge.

"I don't have a clue. Don't you have surveillance cameras throughout the house?"

"Yes, but apparently there was a brief blackout while we were in Belize. Since we weren't here, security wasn't too concerned."

She nodded thoughtfully. That probably meant he didn't suspect she was behind it; at least his ire wasn't with her.

He cut his steak with a fork and knife and continued, "Luckily, José decided to sweep the place in preparation for my uncle's visit this weekend."

Her heart dropped. "Which uncle is coming?" she asked, nervously taking a bite of the delicious dinner Rosa had prepared.

"Enrique."

The food in her mouth suddenly tasted like ash, and she chewed slowly, forcing herself to swallow instead of spit it out in her napkin.

"Oh. I didn't know you'd planned that."

"Yeah, I actually put it on the books just before we left for Belize."

She narrowed her eyes at him. "Why didn't you tell me? When we were talking about it?"

His brows knitted together. "Talking about it? When were we talking about it?"

"When you said you should have a belated birthday party," she quickly exclaimed, noticing the frustration in her voice. She needed to squelch that. Her persona was supposed to be accommodating and demure—although she often forgot and slipped out of character.

Dante grabbed her hand with a patient smile. "Baby, this isn't a birthday party. This is my uncle coming to visit on business. I didn't think I needed to discuss that with you since it really doesn't affect you—although I will expect you to join us for dinner, so maybe I should have."

"No, of course, you don't have to discuss who you invite into your home..."

He cut her off. "Not sure if you've noticed, sweetheart, but it's *our* home now."

Of course she had, and her heart was breaking in two that it was all coming to an end by this weekend. She wasn't ready. She needed more time with him.

Yet, she knew there was no way he was going to want to be with her after she assassinated his uncle. Hell, there was no way the agency would allow her to be with him once she completed her mission. More time with him would only make things harder in the end.

Still, she wanted to cry.

Dante squeezed her hand. "What's the matter, baby?"

She feigned her best debutante smile. "Nothing. I'm just nervous whether or not your uncle will like me. I mean, what if he doesn't?"

"Just be your charming self, and I'm sure everything will be fine."

"I don't have very much time to prepare," she mused. She was going to have to utilize all her free time for prepping this, and Dante hadn't afforded her a lot of spare time lately—not that she'd minded, until now.

"What's to prepare?" he said with an amused smirk.

"The dinner menu, making sure the guest suite is ready, my outfit... I'm going to have to get my hair and nails done. And that's just what I can think of off the top of my head!"

He tilted his head. "I think you're stressing yourself out over nothing. We have staff to handle all the arrangements for his arrival—they've prepared for hundreds of guests over the years: they've gotten quite good at it. Go get your hair and nails done and do some shopping on Friday when he arrives. We'll be busy until dinner. Everything's going to be fine. This really isn't a big deal." He paused, then said quietly, "Is it?"

Ruby swallowed hard. It wasn't like she could say, "Well, I need to figure out how and when I'm going to kill your uncle this weekend; thus ending anything we have. Which is for the best, considering I'm not who you think I am, so yeah, it's kind of a big deal."

She gave a polite smile. "No, of course, you're right. I'm just nervous—I want your family to like me."

****

Dante

He'd come to know her smiles—the ones that were genuine and the ones where she was playing her role—placating him, and the smile she had on her face right now pissed him off. He was going to punish her for it later.

The bugs in his office weren't the only ones on the estate—there were two in his bedroom and several inactivate ones in her closet buried in a secret compartment in one of her purses. He knew those were hers, the ones she originally arrived with but never put to use. That's also why he was confident the ones they'd found today hadn't been planted by her. Plus the timing of it seemed to be while they were gone.

This weekend was obviously going to be a major crossroads in their relationship. She either decided not to go through with her mission, thereby choosing Dante, and if that was the case—he was fucking marrying her before Sunday arrived. Or, she came clean with him, and him with her about the planned coup, and she still followed through with her mission while they figured out a way to make their relationship work. Or, Option C, the one he prayed she didn't choose—she completed her mission and slipped away from him forever. Any scenario's outcome benefitted him but the last one... well, that one would hurt—that much he knew.

He had a feeling which she was going to choose. His birthday weekend had been an epic fantasy—a lovefest of fucking, laughing, and growing closer. If she hadn't confessed everything then, she never would.

Still, he held out hope that when it came down to making a decision, she'd choose him in the end. He guessed he'd find out soon enough.

In the meantime, he was going to spend as much time with—and in—her as he could, reminding her who she really belonged with.

Chapter Twelve

Dante

He stood in the doorway of the library watching her reading, curled up on the chaise by the window. Holding up the wine bottle and glasses he had in his hands, he asked, "Do you want to have some wine by the pool? It's a nice night for a swim."

She looked up from her book and nodded. "That sounds nice. Should I get changed?"

"I don't think that's necessary. We can slip in the water naked." He winked at her and was rewarded with her amused grin as she shook her head.

"How did I know that's what you'd say?"

"Because you know I'd never pass up a chance to get you naked."

Ruby set her book down and stood, walking to where he was waiting. She slid her hands around his waist and looked up at him with a soft smile. "Aw, baby. You know I'll gladly get naked with you anytime."

Dante kissed her forehead then gestured with his head, "Come on."

She sat between his legs while they shared a patio lounger, and he poured them each a glass of wine. Taking a sip, she commented, "This is really good."

"I'm glad you like it. It's from our winery we just bought."

"You own a winery?"

"Well, the family company does. I signed the paperwork an hour before I met you. That's why I'd stopped by the bar that evening to have a celebratory drink."

"You've never told me what your family's company does."

He took a drink as he warred with something. Did he tell her the truth—or at least some semblance of the truth with the hopes that she'd do the same? Had it been fair of him to want her to be honest with him if he hadn't willing to be honest with her—even though he knew that she already knew the truth about him?

"Well, I wasn't exactly lying—what I told you before. I'm the moneyman for the Guzman drug cartel. We do a lot of illegal things, but we're working on phasing in some legal things too."

She was silent. He knew he'd just thrown her for a loop with his honesty and was hoping she was contemplating doing the same thing with him.

Ruby gulped her wine down, still not having said anything in response. Finally, he asked, "Baby? Are you okay? Did you hear me?"

"Yes, I heard you," she whispered. "I don't know how to process what you've just told me." She turned, so she was facing him. "Why would you tell me something like this?"

"It just felt important that if we're going to have a future together that I be honest with you. I want you to know the real me."

She stared at him a long time, her conflict about what to do next was plain as day in her green eyes. He could feel the battle taking place within her, and he found himself holding his breath as he waited for what she was going to do.

Tears filled her eyes, and she whispered, "Dante... I—"

He tucked her hair behind her ear. "Tell me what you're thinking, baby. It's okay."

She was silent again, staring at the water in the pool rather than looking at him. When she finally did return his gaze, it was like he was watching her close down anything she had truly felt. The sadness was evident in her eyes although she offered a weak smile. "I don't know what I'm thinking. This is a lot to wrap my head around."

He nodded silently. The realization this wasn't going to go how he'd hoped slowly sank in. He swung his legs to the edge of the lounger to stand. "I'll give you some space."

She reached for his hand. "No. Don't. Please?"

Her mask was firmly back in place, and he fucking hated it. He had no one but himself to blame for the ache in his heart. He'd known who she was when he started this charade. Getting her to fall in love with him had blown up in his face. He's the one who fell—hard.

He punished her harder that night than he'd had any time before, something she actually seemed to revel in since she begged him not to stop. Maybe it was cathartic for them both—he didn't know.

They didn't discuss the cartel again, and Friday seemed to be looming like an out of control freight train headed toward them at full speed. Dante just didn't know who was going to be on the tracks when the train finally came through.

****

Ruby

His admission about his involvement with the cartel had nearly caused her to confess everything. He'd trusted her—maybe she could do the same with him? But he'd trusted Ruby—an oil heiress who wasn't a threat to his freedom, not Kennedy—a CIA agent.

Was there a there a way for them to be together and have a happily ever after? How would that even be possible? He was a criminal. Everything he was involved in throughout his day-to-day life, she'd devoted her life to fighting. It was a pipe dream—love wasn't going to conquer all. Not for them.

Still, when he'd look at her and smile, she desperately wanted to find a way to make it happen.

As if being able to sense her wavering, her handler sent a report of Enrique's latest exploits—complete with pictures. Headless bodies always bothered her. Decapitating someone was such an intimate act, and she firmly believed you had to be soulless to be able to commit such an atrocity.

Or order it done.

Was Dante involved with such orders? Her heart and gut said no, but that could also just be wishful thinking. Although the intelligence seemed to agree with her.

When Enrique was taken out, there was going to be a power void in the cartel. All reports seemed to indicate Ramon, Enrique's younger brother, was the most likely candidate to fill it, and that Ramon and Dante were aligned. Dante would become even more powerful in the organization. Oddly, knowing that made her decision easier and brought her some comfort. Even though there was no way she could be involved with a criminal for real, maybe there wouldn't be as much brutality if Dante had more influence. Maybe something good could come from her deceit.

Or maybe he'd take his rage over her betrayal out on the world.

Find out what happens next in *Inferno*! Agents of Ensenada—Book One.

https://tesssummersauthor.com/inferno

Other works by Tess Summers:

Inferno
Agents of Ensenada, Book 1

Kennedy Jones

I'm a special agent with the CIA, and I'm good at what I do. In fact, I'm considered one of the best. I can play the role of anyone and eliminating bad guys without them seeing me coming is my forte—which is why I was chosen to take down the head of the Guzman family.

Dante Guzman is a ruthless, sexy, cold-hearted cartel money-man. And now it's my job to study him, learn his likes and dislikes—in and out of the bedroom—so I can gain his trust and access to his uncle, the head of the Ensenada cartel.

I just didn't count on falling into Dante's clutches.

Every second I spend with him he manages to pull me further and further into his world. And the more time I spend there, the deeper I slip into the darkness with him, the more I realize...

I like it.

Dante Guzman

Don't let my good manners fool you—I'm one cold-hearted SOB, and I control the family's monetary affairs with an iron fist. There's no place for weakness in my world. Show weakness, and you die. As simple as that.

So when a petite, feisty, hot-as-hell bombshell storms into my life, I didn't stop to think about the consequences of keeping her. I wanted her, and I always get what I want. Period.

Turns out, the stakes were too high...for the both of us. And there's going to be hell to pay if we're going to be together, to one form of the devil or another.

Get your copy of Inferno!
https://tesssummersauthor.com/inferno

Combustion

Agents of Ensenada, Book 2

She was meant to be mine—I knew it the moment we met. Too bad I'm about to kidnap her.

Mason Hughes

As a decorated CIA agent, I know better than to kidnap a former colleague's sister and hold her hostage on a ship in the middle of the ocean. The agency tends to frown on that sort of behavior. But desperate times call for desperate measures; I have my reasons, and they're good ones. I'll be forgiven with a slap to the wrist—at least for that part of the mission.

Until I tie Reagan Jones up and can't resist her when she presses her tight little body against mine. That's probably not so forgivable.

Then there's the issue of falling in love with her and refusing to let her go once the mission is over. Definitely not forgivable.

I have no idea what I'm thinking—we can't be together; it's not safe for her. I'm a spy, and she's a feisty art instructor from Fargo. Not exactly the perfect match.

Or is it?

Get your copy of Combustion!

https://tesssummersauthor.com/combustion-1

Reignited
Agents of Ensenada, Book 3

He's known as the CIA's top mercenary fixer. But he can't fix this.

Jacob Smith

Seven years.

Seven long miserable years since he'd ripped his heart from his chest and left it on her doorstep when he walked away from her. But, he'd had no choice.

At least, he'd thought he hadn't. He was too entrenched in the CIA's underground world to safely ever have a wife and family.

But now, after turning his CIA dealings into a *very* lucrative mercenary career, here he was, about to embark on a ten-day cruise with his cabin next to hers, not by coincidence—although she didn't know it yet.

He wasn't known as a 'fixer' for nothing. Maybe it was time to try to fix his broken heart, and hers—if she'd let him. And that was a big *if*, given how he'd shattered hers so long ago.

Reignited is Book Three in the Agents of Ensenada series. Each book is a standalone, with a guaranteed HEA and no cliffhangers.

https://tesssummersauthor.com/reignited

San Diego Social Scene series

The Boston's Elite Series

Acknowledgements

Renee Rose—Thank you for beta reading and offering your always sage advice. I love you, woman!

Simone Elise—Thank you for making this book better with your edits. I freaking hate commas so much.

OliviaProDesigns—another amazing cover.

Steph Armstrong, Jill Garrett, and all the Tess Summers' Sizzling Playhouse Group—you guys are the reason I even log onto Facebook these days. Thanks for making our group such a fun, upbeat place to hang out.

My dear readers—Thank you for letting me continue to do what I love doing every day and for loving my characters as much as I do.

Last, but not least, Mr. Summers—25 years is a long time to have to legally put up with me. Thanks for always making me feel special. It's been a fun ride and am looking forward to the next twenty-five.

About the Author

Tess Summers is a former businesswoman and teacher who always loved writing but never seemed to have time to sit down and write a short story, let alone a novel. Now battling MS, her life changed dramatically, and she has finally slowed down enough to start writing all the stories she's been wanting to tell, including the fun and sexy ones!

Married over twenty-five years with three grown children, Tess is a former dog foster mom who ended up failing and adopting them instead. She and her husband (and their six dogs) split their time between the desert of Arizona and the lakes of Michigan, so she's always in a climate that's not too hot and not too cold, but just right!

Contact Me!

Sign up for my newsletter: BookHip.com/SNGBXD

Email: TessSummersAuthor@yahoo.com

Visit my website: www.TessSummersAuthor.com

Facebook: http://facebook.com/TessSummersAuthor

Instagram: https://www.instagram.com/tesssummers/

Amazon: https://amzn.to/2MHHhdK

BookBub https://www.bookbub.com/profile/tess-summers

My FB Group: Tess Summers Sizzling Playhouse

TikTok: https://www.tiktok.com/@tesssummersauthor

Goodreads - https://www.goodreads.com/TessSummers

www.ingramcontent.com/pod-product-compliance
Lightning Source LLC
Chambersburg PA
CBHW051927110726
47902CB00002B/445